The Mysterious V

Volume. II

Sophia Reeve

Alpha Editions

This edition published in 2024

ISBN : 9789361470202

Design and Setting By
Alpha Editions
www.alphaedis.com
Email - info@alphaedis.com

As per information held with us this book is in Public Domain.
This book is a reproduction of an important historical work. Alpha Editions uses the best technology to reproduce historical work in the same manner it was first published to preserve its original nature. Any marks or number seen are left intentionally to preserve its true form.

Contents

CHAPTER I. ....- 1 -
CHAPTER II. ....- 10 -
CHAPTER III. ....- 18 -
CHAPTER IV. ....- 29 -
CHAPTER V. ....- 41 -
CHAPTER VI. ....- 48 -
CHAPTER VII. ....- 55 -

CHAPTER I.

Sir Henry entertained not the least doubt of its being Ferrand who had taken Louise; nor, from his general character, but that he would endeavour to retain her, though in open defiance to the Governor's command. That he was devoid of principle or honour, he had given an indubitable proof, in his intended assassination of Harland; nor would the affair, Sir Henry apprehended, yet end without an effusion of blood. The courage of Sir Henry was cool but constant: an injury offered to himself, the benevolence of his disposition would induce him rather to pardon than resent; but this outrage to a sister he sincerely loved affected him more keenly; and he determined, should Ferrand prove the aggressor, to hazard, or even lose his life, to effect her liberation. With his mind absorbed in a labyrinth of conjectures, and plans for his procedure, he arrived at the Governor's country residence, and, on inquiring for Ferrand, was shown into a library.

The East-Indian received him with a constrained civility; which, however, ceased on learning the purport of his visit: and, in answer to Sir Henry's demand, if his sister were there? he haughtily replied, he was not answerable to any one for his conduct, nor would he be questioned like a school-boy, or dictated to!

"It is not my intention, Sir," said Sir Henry loftily, "to dictate to you; for my question, if you refuse to answer it, your servants, I doubt not, will give the information I want: if not, I shall proceed to the executive part of my commission."

Ferrand bit his lip, and, stamping with passion, exclaimed, "What farther insults am I to receive? I have been rejected by a proud menial; my love contemned; insulted by a rival; reproved for my just vengeance, and treated as a prisoner!—and now—on what authority is the finger of suspicion pointed at me? Search the fleet; you may, perhaps, find her with some of her gallant countrymen!"

As he uttered the last sentence, he flung from the room, leaving Sir Henry to proceed as he should think proper. Sir Henry was not long in determining: he summoned the attendants, and, showing the Governor's order, demanded to be admitted into every apartment. But Louise was not to be found; and Sir Henry at last was persuaded she was not in the power of Ferrand. The suspicion too that she might have been torn away by some of the French officers who daily visited the Marchioness, added to his perplexity. Had Ferrand, he thought, been guilty, he would rather have braved the action; but, on the contrary, he appeared wholly actuated by rage at his restriction.

Uncertain how to act, or where to proceed to recover Louise, he returned to the Marchioness's, where the impatient Harland had unwillingly remained. His countenance told the success of his commission; and scarcely could his tongue confirm it, ere Harland exclaimed—"I knew it—I knew it! Fool that I was to yield to the command of an interested dotard, and idly lose the moments which may have teemed with danger to her. But I will find her, though hell and earth combine to hide her from me!"

He rushed out of the house, followed by Sir Henry, who asked which way he proposed to direct his course?—"The island is before me," answered Harland distractedly, "nor will I leave a single spot unsearched!"

Sir Henry mentioned the suspicion to which Ferrand had given rise, and proposed requesting of the Governor that an inquiry might be made through the fleets. Harland eagerly agreed to the measure; to which the Governor as readily consented. Commissioners were accordingly deputed to the several vessels, whilst Harland and Sir Henry, after vainly searching the town, directed their course to the surrounding plantations: but disappointment still attended them; the lovely fugitive was no where to be discovered, though the most liberal rewards were offered to those who could give intelligence respecting her.

For four days they continued their search, scarcely allowing themselves the rest and refreshment nature required, when, to add to their distress, they were informed the fleet was ready to sail, and only waited for a favourable wind.

"God of Heaven prevent it!" exclaimed Harland, "for if Louise be not found, I can sooner forfeit my commission, my honour, nay my life, than lose her! What can be done, Sir Henry? Which way can we go?"

"Chance, or rather Providence, George," answered Sir Henry dejectedly, "must direct us. Though the unfortunate girl I am afraid is too well secreted to be discovered by any means we can use."

"Drive me not mad, Sir Henry, by the supposition," said Harland; "rather encourage me with hopes, though delusive ones, than tear my heart by such a truth."

"Alas, Harland," answered Sir Henry, "I would encourage hope in you, but it is dead in my own bosom. Louise, I am afraid, is irrecoverably lost."

"I must not, will not lose her," cried the frantic Harland. "Ferrand, the villain Ferrand, too surely has her in his power! But I will instantly go to the grove, despite of his uncle's prohibition, and force the truth from him."

He turned into a path which conducted to the Governor's seat, and Sir Henry, after a moment's hesitation, followed him. "I will go with you, Harland," he said; "if Louise be secreted at the Grove, my assistance may be requisite; and the Governor, in that respect, I doubt not, will pardon our transgressing the bounds he has prescribed. If she be not, my presence will be equally necessary, as your passion may otherwise hurry you into too great excesses."

They were here interrupted by the appearance of a skirmish in an adjoining enclosure; and, on their nearer approach, beheld an old negro defending himself with a stake against four others who were armed. The odds were too great to demand a moment's hesitation how to act: they hastened to his rescue, and, after a slight contest, compelled their opponents to retreat. Sir Henry then directed his attention to the old man, who had fallen to the ground apparently lifeless.

"The poor wretch, I believe, is dying," said Harland, as he assisted Sir Henry to raise him, "and here no assistance can be had." Sir Henry supported him against his knee. The negro faintly opened his eyes, and regarded them with a wild surprise, which, as recollection returned, gradually settled to a look of stern ferocity.

"How can we remove him?" said Sir Henry, "To leave him thus is impossible."

"To take him with us is equally impossible," answered Harland, impatiently, "and the day, Corbet, wears apace."

"Yet cannot I leave him to perish," said Sir Henry. "Try, my good fellow, if you can walk or stand."

"Let me die where I am," answered the negro sullenly.

"Leave him—leave him, Sir Henry," exclaimed Harland; "Louise is of more consequence than a worthless runaway slave, for such I am certain he is; and to her, I think, a brother's hand ought to be extended."

"And shall be, Harland," said Sir Henry, with emotion. "Yet, as a man, is this slave my brother, and to him shall my hand be extended also. I feel the weight of his afflictions, the misery of his life passed in slavery; and, with him, could curse the hand that first forged chains for a fellow-creature!—A few minutes, and he may be better; and we will then prosecute our search for my unfortunate Louise."

During this speech the old negro had raised himself from the knee of Sir Henry, and grasped his arm, with that anxious confidence the unhappy only can feel when relieved by the hand of benevolence; each word struck as a chord on his heart, and told him he was supported by a friend.—"Seek you Louise de St. Ursule?" he hesitatingly asked. The quick ear of Harland caught the sound, and, springing toward him, he demanded if he knew aught of

Louise? "I do," answered the slave, with reserve, "and if this European seek her, will direct him to her."

"Tell me this instant," said Harland; "on your life I charge you!"

"You may take it, if you please," said the negro coolly, "and afterward find her if you can. I am a slave, and, as you said, a runaway! If I discover the European woman to you, in return, perhaps, you would deliver me to a merciless master, to expire beneath the whip."

Harland deserved not the supposition; cruelty formed no part of his character, though truly the child of pride. Unused to entreat, he had demanded the information he would not have regretted half his fortune to have obtained. The answer of the slave stung him to the heart; and, though Louise was at stake, he would have retorted with the wildest acrimony, had not Sir Henry prevented him, by saying to the slave—"If you be the means of restoring Louise to us, I promise to procure your pardon, if the interest of the Governor can effect it; and your liberty, if your owner will dispose of you."

The slave half rose, looked wistfully in the face of Sir Henry: the name of liberty sounded sweetly on his ear, and made his heart beat with unwonted velocity. Yet a momentary doubt shot across his brain. Mankind had ever been his enemy; could he then give credit to the flattering promise?—The countenance of Sir Henry beamed with philanthropy and truth; suspicion vanished; and, rising from the ground, he cried—"I will believe you.—Pursue the path you are in, and I will conduct you to her."

"You forget your late accident," said Sir Henry; "let me assist you."

"I am, I believe," said the old man, "more capable of walking than you. Slavery has inured me to fatigue. Neither am I materially hurt. I was exhausted when you came to my assistance, and stunned by the last blow I received. But your timely interposition saved my life, and freely now shall you command it."

He conducted them, by private paths, to a plantation near Ferrand Grove; in which, after some time, he pointed out a small cottage, so concealed by the foliage that it might have escaped the eyes of a casual observer.—"I can proceed no farther," he said, "without danger of being seen and retaken, which would inevitably bring me to a merciless death. There is the cottage I yester-evening fled from; and there is Louise de St. Ursule confined."

Harland heard no more, but rushed through a gateway which opened to the cottage. The soft voice of Louise, broken by a plaintive sob, reached his ear; and, a moment after, that of Ferrand, speaking in a threatening tone. With a resistless force, the maddened effort of the moment, he burst the door, and the next instant brought him to the presence of Louise and his rival.

Ferrand started at the unexpected apparition, but drew his sword, perceiving the point of Harland's already at his breast; whilst Louise, with a scream of mingled joy and terror, attempted to throw herself into the protecting arms of her lover; but was withheld by one of Ferrand's attendants, who, recalling to mind his master's assailant, endeavoured to force her to the interior part of the cottage. In this he was prevented by Sir Henry, who had followed Harland, and who now sprung to the rescue of his sister. A few minutes would have decided the conflict in favour of the adventurers, but the domestics, alarmed by the tumult and the screams of Louise, hastened to the assistance of their master. They were, therefore, obliged to act on the defensive; and, to add to their distress, Louise, after vainly struggling for emancipation, sunk senseless at the feet of Ferrand. Another moment and she had been torn from their sight; when Ferrand, thrown off his guard by her fall, received a wound from Harland: he staggered—and the servant, who was raising the fair cause of the contention, extended his arm to save his master. It was a moment granted by fortune. Quick as lightning Sir Henry tore her from him, and, defended by Harland, conveyed her out of the cottage. By the time they had passed the gate, Ferrand, however, was sufficiently recovered to order the servants, who had officiously attended to him, to pursue them, and force Louise back. They hastened to execute his commands, but the narrowness of the path prevented their passing to impede the flight of the fugitives. The sword of Harland was opposed to those who first presented themselves; but fearing they would force their way through the underwood, and thus surround them, he hastily bade Sir Henry—save Louise! Sir Henry, accordingly, after an anxious but vain look for the old negro, and desiring the Lieutenant to follow him, entered the nearly trackless path by which they had been conducted to the cottage.

Louise soon revived; and, after a few incoherent exclamations of joy, and thankfulness at her deliverance, anxiously inquired after Harland. "I hope in a few minutes he will join us," answered Sir Henry. But scarcely were the words pronounced when they heard a violent tumult, and immediately after distinguished the voice of Ferrand, commanding his people to pursue Louise. His anxiety for George was instantly absorbed in apprehension for the safety of his sister, and, supporting her on his arm, they again fled.

Night soon concealed them from farther danger, and the hapless Harland retook possession of their imaginations. The timid Louise, with tearful eyes, endeavoured to pierce through the gloom, or entreated Sir Henry to stop and listen if perchance his distant footfall, or voice, could be heard. But all was silent—and busy fancy quickly portrayed him as sinking beneath the vengeance of his furious rival. Sir Henry's thoughts did not present a more cheerful picture; he entertained not a doubt but Ferrand had overpowered the Lieutenant; and an idea of assassination presented itself to his imagination, which the ferocious character of the East-Indian but too justly authorised. Could he have left Louise, he would instantly have retraced his way to the cottage, but no friendly roof presented itself which might have afforded shelter for the lovely maid; he had therefore no alternative but to proceed, though every nerve trembling with anxiety to return and aid the unfortunate Lieutenant.

It was nearly the hour of midnight when they arrived at the Marchioness's, where Louise had again the satisfaction of being folded to the bosom of her generous benefactress. An inquiry after Harland followed the embrace. The tears of Louise informed her some accident had happened; and, on her applying to Sir Henry for an explanation, he gave a concise relation of the evening's adventures; at the same time declaring his intention of instantly returning. The Marchioness could not oppose his determination, but applied herself to console Louise, who appeared nearly overpowered by her emotions.

Sir Henry advanced to her, and tenderly taking her hand—"Indulge not this immoderate grief, my dear girl, which can only add to our present distress. Summon your fortitude. George may be wounded—he may be overpowered; or, which is most probable, he may have missed his way in the plantations. I yesterday, my dear girl, despaired of ever beholding you again; yet, when least expected, Providence conducted us to you. Hope, then, for the best. I will proceed, with the utmost expedition, to his assistance, if he need it: and if our fears are prophetic—but you must not indulge the idea.—Harland shall live, and live to bless my Louise!"

The enthusiasm with which Sir Henry pronounced the last sentence, imparted a hope to the heart of Louise, he dared not himself indulge. She faintly smiled through her tears: Sir Henry again repeated—"Hope for the best!" and was hastening out of the room, when a loud peal at the outward door arrested his steps, and, the minute after, Harland, with breathless impatience, rushed into the room, followed by the old Negro.

"My dearest, loveliest girl!" he exclaimed, clasping the delighted Louise to his bosom; "am I again so blessed as to behold you?—Nor will I part from you again, my Louise, till the Church's sanction has placed it beyond the power of aught but death to separate us!"

"But you are wounded, Harland," said the Marchioness anxiously; "let me procure you some assistance."

Harland, indeed, had forgotten his wounds, and the joy Louise at first experienced on seeing him, prevented her observing his pallid countenance, or the blood which had stained his clothes. She now with trembling lips joined in the Marchioness's request, that a surgeon might be sent for. Harland complied,—"though the hurts I have received," he continued, "are not such as to require a moment's consideration. But the dastardly villain, Sir Henry, who inflicted them, shall yet feel the power of my arm!"

The last words were uttered with a vehemence which declared Ferrand not only the man alluded to, but that he had been guilty of some atrocity they were as yet unacquainted with.

"Ah, Harland!" sighed Louise, "if you have any regard for my peace, resign all thoughts of revenge, in which perhaps yourself, not Ferrand, might become the victim!"

"In every other circumstance of my life," said Harland, "Louise shall be my monitor; but I cannot tamely pass by the injuries I have received. To Sir Henry I am indebted for your preservation—to yonder slave for my own!—Not two hours since he saved me from the assassin's hand!"

The countenance of Louise assumed a paler hue at this relation.—"Yonder slave!" she faintly repeated.—"It is the villain who forced me to the cottage of Ferrand."

The old slave, who had hitherto remained near the door, now advanced:—"I am, it is true, Madam," he said, "the man who, by the commands of an imperious master, took you from your friends: yet am I not deserving the name of villain! The slave—but not the man, was guilty of the action!—By preserving you from dishonour, I incurred the usage which drove me a naked fugitive from my ancient home. These Europeans saved me from a cruel death, and promised the richest reward a wretched slave could receive, if I would conduct them to you. I did more—and let the action prove a Negro's soul to be susceptible of gratitude!"

Louise blushed her recantation of the sentiments she had entertained respecting the slave. "You have raised my curiosity," said the Marchioness, "to the highest degree: but as I am certain my Louise, and you, my young friends, are greatly in need of repose; I will repress it till the morning, when I shall expect to have it gratified by an ample relation of every incident."

Louise thankfully acceded to the Marchioness's proposal of retiring, and again took possession of her former apartment; whither one of the Marchioness's daughters accompanied her, that no farther attempt might be made, without the knowledge of the family or the means of assistance. Harland likewise, after a surgeon had attended him, retired, as did Sir Henry, to the apartments which had been prepared for them, and where repose, the sweetest they had long experienced, rewarded them for the toils and anxieties of the day.

It was late in the morning when they assembled at the breakfast-table; where the Captain and Frederick, having been previously informed of the successful termination of Sir Henry and Harland's search, attended them. Mutual compliments and congratulations passed, and after breakfast the Marchioness reminded them of the last night's arrangement, and Louise began her relation, as follows:

"I had not, my dear Madam, retired many minutes to my apartment, on the night I was forced away, when Rachel, (who has chiefly attended on me since our arrival in St. Helena) after apologizing for the liberty she was going to take, with a well-counterfeited appearance of concern, began to relate a tale of a distressed family, highly deserving, she said, of compassion and relief, who wished to apply for your beneficence, but wanted a friend to speak for them: and, knowing my influence, she had given her word, she said, to ask my assistance.

"I inquired more particularly into the nature of their distress; and she so insensibly engaged my attention by her interesting but artful tale, that the time passed unheeded till long after the usual hour of repose. I was first recalled to a sense of my improper conduct, by a light footstep on the outside of my apartment. Unsuspicious of danger, I was hastening to see who it was, and to apologize, if by my heedlessness I had disturbed any part of the family; when two men entered the room, and before I could call for help, Rachel threw a handkerchief over my head, which she tied so securely across my mouth, that the power of speech was entirely prevented. My struggles were equally inefficacious: my hands and feet were bound, and I was then carried silently down the stairs, and conveyed to the cottage of Ferrand; where freeing me from my bonds, they left me to reflections painful in the highest degree. The idea that they designed to murder me, which had taken possession of my mind on our first entrance into the plantation, then gave place to fears far better founded, and I dreaded the moment which would bring Ferrand to my sight.

"An old female soon attended, to show me to a chamber: I endeavoured to interest her in my favour, and to prevail on her to aid me in returning to my friends. But she heard me with indifference, spoke in praise of Ferrand, who, she said, would visit me in the evening, and, advising me to seek repose, again left me. Thankful, and somewhat easier by hearing Ferrand was not under the same roof with me, I determined to take advantage of the respite allowed, and if possible effect my escape. I hastened to the window—it was secured by strong iron bars, and the door had been locked and bolted on the outside by my female gaoler. Disappointed in the faint hope I entertained of liberty, I yielded to a momentary despair, and, bursting into tears, threw myself on the bed. Reflection, however, soon showed me the inutility of my grief: many hours were to pass before Ferrand would come to the cottage; I therefore endeavoured to calm my agitation, that I might, if possible, meet him with firmness and resolution. Then again I dreaded the uncontrolled licence of his passions, or that Harland or my brother, learning who had taken me away, might be involved in a quarrel, which would terminate in the loss of their lives.

"It was noon when my attendant entered with refreshments; and a smile, I thought truly demoniacal, played on her features as she again launched out in praise of her master, and the happy life I might lead if I were but compliant with his wishes. I listened to her in silence, as my spirits were too dejected to permit my answering her; and she left me, I believe highly satisfied with her own eloquence. The afternoon passed comfortless; evening arrived; and I was forced from reflections on a more deserving lover, to the presence of Ferrand. He accosted me with an exultation and assurance that implied he thought the conquest over me completely gained, by the success of his stratagem: he did not, therefore, patiently listen to my reproaches and animadversions on his conduct; but, after a violent paroxysm of passion, reminded me he was then the master of my fate. He was willing, he said, to join his destiny with mine by a lawful union; but, if I rejected his offer, I must answer to myself for any measures he might pursue. I could not conceal the terror occasioned by this declaration; the courage I at first exerted forsook me, and tears and entreaties were my only defence. The next day, and the next, passed with little variation; Ferrand sometimes strove to soothe, but more often to terrify me to compliance. The third evening a violent bustle in the lower rooms raised my hopes that my brother and Harland had gained intelligence of my prison, and were come to my deliverance. With a throbbing heart I listened to catch the welcome sound of their voices; but the tumult gradually ceased; all became quiet; and I was obliged to resign myself to a state rendered more horrid by the short-lived but sanguine hope I had indulged of liberation.

"I did not see Ferrand again till late the next day; when he informed me the fleets had sailed, and that Harland and my friends had left the island. I cannot attempt to describe the agony of mind I endured on receiving this intelligence. He renewed his offer of immediate marriage, but I turned from him with horror. My sorrow renewed his anger; he repeated his threats—declared he would grant me only till the morning to determine whether I would accept his honourable proposal, or submit to a state of infamy; and was proceeding in his invectives, when the door was burst from its hinges, and the entrance of my Harland and Sir Henry proved the falsity of Ferrand's report, and changed my sorrow to joy."

CHAPTER II.

Louise ceased speaking, and Harland, who had with difficulty restrained his impatience during the latter part of her relation, exclaimed—"And think you, my Louise, I will not chastise the villain for his conduct?—I should be undeserving the affection you have honoured me with to let it pass unpunished!"

The Marchioness smiled.—"At present, Harland, we will think of your marriage with Louise. You have sufficiently proved your knight-errantry by her rescue: and as for Ferrand, I think he is punished enough, in the loss of his mistress, for the steps he took to obtain her. Had you, my young friend, been the rejected lover, I do not think your passions would have been more under control than his have been."

Harland looked confused. The Captain returned the Marchioness's smile. "Harland, I believe, Madam, feels the force of the words you have uttered: and let their plain truth, George, recommend them to your consideration. Your character for courage has been long established: but that courage, if it lead you to revenge, degenerates to assassination; nor could I then regard you in a more respectable light than the hired Bravo! Too much blood has already been shed. Leave Ferrand then to the dictate of his own conscience for what he has done, and yield to the happiness which awaits you. Our stay here may be limited to a few hours, and it is highly necessary your union with Mademoiselle St. Ursule should take place before we part with the Marchioness."

The latter part of this speech reconciled George to its preceding reproof; and he earnestly entreated the marriage might take place that very evening.

"To-morrow morning it shall," said the Marchioness; "but some little preparation is necessary: our worthy friend the Governor is not yet acquainted with our Louise's return: and one piece of justice yet remains to be performed: Rachel ought not, nor shall she escape punishment, for her assistance toward the destruction of Louise."

The lovely girl here interceded for the guilty Rachel; who, she said, had certainly been bribed by Ferrand to the action. "That very consideration," the Marchioness replied, "added to her guilt; as it proved her ingratitude to a generous mistress." And as Sir Henry and his friends sided with the Marchioness, Louise was obliged to submit.

Rachel was therefore ordered to appear; but, after repeated summonses, was declared to have absconded! On the return of Louise she indeed became certain the part she had taken in betraying her to Ferrand must be discovered; and, to avoid punishment, she secretly conveyed her clothes to the house of a friend, and early in the morning departed for the cottage. The Marchioness was therefore necessitated to leave her punishment to the future vigilance and justice of the Governor; to whom a servant was dispatched to acquaint him with Sir Henry and Harland's success: and composure being once more restored, that lady reminded Harland his evening adventures were yet to be related. George bowed, and immediately began:

"I guarded the pass from the cottage, my dear Madam, till my Louise was out of sight; when I endeavoured also to retreat, and should have succeeded, had not Ferrand (recovered from the effects of our late rencounter) come from the cottage. Perceiving my sweet girl was escaped, he turned the effects of his rage against me, who did not patiently receive the onset; and a far more furious contest than the former commenced. Blinded by rage against my principal adversary, I too much disregarded the number and power of his servants, who then found means to surround me, and treacherously assailed me behind. In consequence of this I was overpowered and dragged to the ground. 'Secure him!' was all Ferrand uttered, as he darted past me, with some of his servants, to pursue Sir Henry. His orders, however, were punctually obeyed by those who remained, and I was in an instant effectually secured.

"You, my friends, who so well know my irritable temper, may judge of my rage at the restriction and indignity I endured. The only power I retained was that of speech, and I vented my passion in vain defiance and imprecations against Ferrand. After some time I was carried into the cottage; and thence again removed to a rude cave or grot in a retired part of the plantation: a place apparently formed for murder and the blackest deeds; and where I was left on a few rushes to exhaust the residue of my rage.

"Some time elapsed, when Ferrand presented himself, with a light in one hand, his sword in the other; fury and madness were depicted in his countenance, and reflected with additional force by the red glare of the torch.

"'You—scoundrel, at least, have not escaped me!' he vociferated as he advanced, 'and shall now pay for the slights and indignities I have endured! For you, Louise rejected me; and has placed a serpent in my heart: but some of its stings shall yet reach her in the person of her minion!'

"My satisfaction at the certainty of Louise's escape, was absorbed in returning fury at this address. I struggled to shake off my fetters; demanded to be free; and that our pretensions might be ultimately decided by the sword!

"'They shall be!' he repeated with increased vehemence. His hand was raised to plunge his sword into my bosom, when the old slave darted from the entrance, and, before its point could reach me, arrested his arm! A scuffle ensued: but Ferrand was by no means able to contend with his slave; who soon wrested the sword from him.—

"'Villain! Degenerate wretch!' he exclaimed, nearly choked with rage, 'thy life shall answer for this interference!'

"'My life!' repeated the old man, grasping him firmly by the collar and shaking him. 'Thine is now completely in my power!—and here may I revenge the blows, the usage, thou hast unjustly dealt me: but I scorn to embrue my hands in thy blood. Begone!—and thank the mercy of thy slave, thou art not now grovelling in the dust!'

"He cast him to the entrance, and Ferrand, who had shrunk with terror when in the hands of the stern negro, hastened toward the cottage, calling for help, and vociferating the names of his servants. The old man snatched up the torch, which lay burning on the ground, and, placing it in the earth, hastily applied himself to extricate me from the fetters with which I had been loaded. Fully sensible of the inevitable death he had preserved me from, I endeavoured to express the gratitude which swelled in my heart, and promised not only to join with Sir Henry in procuring his liberty, but to add such a recompense as should evince my sense of the obligation I owed him.

"'To Sir Henry, and the European woman,' he replied, 'you are indebted for your preservation. From what I over-heard, I learned you were the friend of one, the destined husband of the other: and, for their sakes, was I coming to liberate you, when the haughty Ferrand passed me: and let the danger you have been in teach you this lesson—never to scorn a fellow-creature, or despise his afflictions, because he is beneath you. The lowest weed you carelessly trample on, is not without its virtues; and is equally the work of the Creator as the loftiest pine of the forest. As men, we all are equal: nor are the circumstances of life so certain, but the monarch may be indebted for his existence to the hand of a slave!' He raised me from the ground; and, as a sentiment of shame arose for the cause of this reproach, I accepted his proffered arm in silence, for my limbs were at first too benumbed to admit of my walking without assistance. The voice of Ferrand, directing his servants as he again approached the recess, informed us not a moment was to be lost; and my companion, dashing out the torch, with hasty steps conducted me into the plantation. By paths well known to himself, he guided me across the tangled wilderness to the high road, where he first broke silence, by informing me we were out of danger. We, however, continued our way with the utmost expedition, as my soul burned with impatience to be convinced that my beloved Louise was not only freed from the power of Ferrand, but that she was also safe under the protection of her amiable benefactress."

The comments on this account of Harland, were interrupted by the arrival of the Governor, who, after congratulating him on the recovery of Louise, likewise requested to be informed of the particulars respecting her disappearance and restoration. Louise and Harland therefore briefly recapitulated the foregoing events; Harland only enlarging on those circumstances wherein the old slave was concerned. The Governor listened with attention to their relations, and with visible concern and impatience to what had passed in the cave. When Harland concluded, he appeared for some moments absorbed in reflection, and then desired to see the slave. Sir Henry and Harland looked anxiously at each other, and would have interceded in behalf of the old man, but were prevented by his entrance; their apprehensions on his account, however, ceased, as the Governor said—

"So, Carlo—I find you have been a principal actor in the adventures of our European friends. You have undoubtedly acted right as a man, but not with the obedience and respect due from a slave to his owner. I am, however, so well pleased with the termination of this affair, I rather wish to reward than punish you. For your preservation of this gentleman, I therefore pardon your desertion: for your forbearance on the life of my Ferrand, I give you your liberty!"

"Liberty—liberty!" shouted the old man; "oh, bless my ears with a repetition of the word! Say again that I am free, and I will indeed believe you!"

"From this moment," repeated the Governor, "I declare you free; and these your friends are witnesses of that declaration."

Carlo sunk at the feet of his generous master; embraced his knees; and, whilst the tears of gratitude rolled down his cheeks, in broken accents breathed his thanks. The Governor appeared affected—

"At how easy a price," he cried, addressing the Captain, "might man, would he reflect, dispense happiness on a fellow-creature. I declare, till this moment I never felt the irresistible power of nature, or how nearly allied the free man was to the slave. Rise, Carlo; I will make it my business to provide for you in a manner more suitable to your deserts."

"That," said Harland, "shall be my care. The obligations I am under to Carlo, can never be repaid; but I will instantly assign over to him, property to the value of two thousand pounds, as an acknowledgment for the services he has rendered me, and as a peace-offering for the sentiments I once expressed; and if he will go with me to England, I will settle him to his satisfaction, either in a mercantile or agricultural situation."

Carlo rose from the feet of his late master, and grasping Harland's arm, said energetically—"I thank you!—my heart feels your bounty, but I cannot speak its sentiments. Not to England, however, do I wish to go. Give me half the wealth you have named, and let me return to Coromandel; the land where first I drew my breath; the land whence, ere fourteen revolving seasons had marked my life, I was basely torn from freedom, friends, and kindred!—but I beg your pardon; in this moment when my soul is overflowing with joy—

with gratitude—I ought not to intrude a tale of misery, or vex your ears with woes which no longer exist."

"I have often, Carlo," said the Governor, "thought you superior to a common slave; but the duties of my situation, and my own more immediate concerns, prevented my ever questioning you on the subject; but as the late events have introduced you more particularly to our notice, these your friends, I doubt not, will excuse my inquiring by what accident you were forced into slavery?"

"Forced indeed!" ejaculated Carlo. "For till then I was gay and free as the breeze which lightly fanned my native groves.—I had one day, Sir, been with some of my youthful companions, laving my limbs in the expanded ocean, when a party of European sailors came to the spot where we were: they found us unarmed—an easy prey; and, seizing us in spite of resistance, forced us on board their vessel, and brought us to this island, where we were consigned to slavery! It is true, my chains for years were formed with flowers. The late Governor became my master; and when memory brought to mind the past, or painted the distraction of my parents for my loss—if I madly reprobated the hand that tore me from them, or sunk in despondence, wept, and sighed for liberty; he would deign to soothe my sorrows; on hearing my tale, he did more: he promised to restore me to my friends and country! But alas—grief for the loss of her offspring, had closed the number of my mother's days; my father sought his child, to redeem him—and perished in the search!

"My generous benefactor, on being informed of these events, declared he would in future supply the place of the parents I had lost; I should be the child of his adoption, and as such he would provide for me. I was accordingly instructed in those sciences by which Europeans claim superiority over ruder climes; and never had he cause to regret his beneficence. At his death, he said, I should be free and affluent; nay, would then have given me liberty, but that he feared to lose me. Ah! he knew not, that the strongest chains which can be forged, are those of gratitude and affection!

"His death happened too suddenly for him to fulfil his intentions in my favour; and his sordid relations, who had long regarded me with jealous envy, sold me with the rest of his slaves!

"Then indeed I first experienced the horrors of slavery: those who had courted my acquaintance in the days of prosperity, when it was no longer in my power to render them services, ceased to know me: my friendship was no longer sought—I was disregarded—forgotten! Till then, hope had cheered my days and shed her influence on my slumbers; she then deserted me—and each succeeding day was marked with misery!

"Many, indeed, have been my afflictions: nor do I count the loss of an humble, but faithful companion, who was rudely torn from my arms, the least I have endured. After twenty years absence, I was once more brought to St. Helena, and bought, my noble master, by you. But far different was I from what I had been in the days of my youth: affliction had gradually marked my brow with gloom, and deadened the milder virtues of my heart! I was appointed by you, to attend on your nephew; who—but he had never experienced woe; how then could he judge of that, he wantonly inflicted on others!

"By him I was commanded, with his favourite valet, to force Mademoiselle de St. Ursule to the cottage; which was easily effected with the assistance of Rachel. The sight of her, I could not but regard as a victim, rekindled a spark of pity in my bosom: that she disliked your nephew and loved another, I had discovered in his moments of passion; I thought of the wife who had been forced from me: a pang shot through my heart, and I wished if possible to save her: but Marguerite too well knew the duties of her office, to entrust the keys of her chamber in my possession.

"The offers of your nephew were rejected by that lady; and on the third day of her confinement, he vowed, by force or stratagem, to effect his purpose. The sibyl of his pleasures proposed drugs, which she accordingly prepared, and mixed in a beverage for the lovely prisoner. The indignation of my soul could then be no longer restrained. I dashed the vessel to the floor, and, forgetting I was his slave, reproved him for his ungenerous proceedings!

"What followed, I scarcely need relate: he struck me, and, summoning my fellow slaves, ordered me to be punished—even to death! But indignation gave me strength, I broke from them, and sought refuge among the rocks. My enraged master, as I yester-evening learned, joined himself in the fruitless pursuit, he ordered after me.

"The remembrance of the lady whom I wished to save, returned with the morning; I thought I might perhaps be able to effect her deliverance, or at least inform her friends where she was; and for that purpose was, toward the close of the day, retracing my steps to the plantation which surrounds the cottage, and where I thought I might lie concealed, when I was suddenly attacked by four of my late companions, and but for the assistance of these gentlemen, should there have resigned my being! They, however, preserved me, and with you, have this day restored me to life—to hope—to happiness! My faithful Mella bears her bonds in my native land, and thither would I return, that she too may be free; and with me hourly offer up her prayers for those, whose beneficence had unbound the chains of our slavery!"

"And you shall return, Carlo," said the Marchioness, "if I have any influence with these gentlemen. I am going to Pondicherry; and you shall return with me. The present of your generous young friend will be sufficient to establish you; and under the protection of my husband, the Governor, you yet may experience the happiness you so truly deserve."

The Governor and Harland readily agreed to the Marchioness's arrangement; and Carlo retired, anticipating with impatience the hour which would restore him to his native land, and his long-lost Mella.

The Governor soon after took his leave, as did the Captain, who, with Frederick and Sir Henry, returned on board: Harland only remaining at the Marchioness's.

At last the hour so ardently wished for arrived, which was to unite the lovely Louise to Harland. Sir Henry and his friends attended: the Governor likewise honoured the ceremony with his presence, and by his generous behaviour endeavoured to atone for his former restriction on George, which the well-known disposition of his nephew (who had shut himself up in gloomy discontent at the Grove) rendered highly necessary. A numerous company had been invited to pass the day at the Marchioness's, not only in honour of Louise's nuptials, but also as a farewell visit, the next day being appointed for their embarkation. The thoughts of separation, however, were superseded by the pleasure which prevailed, and animated every countenance.

In the course of the evening, Sir Henry, who by the friendship of the Captain had procured a draft on a merchant at Pondicherry, for a thousand pounds, sought Carlo, and, taking him into a private room, presented him with it, saying—"I must beg your acceptance, Carlo, of this mark of my friendship. I believe I possess a place in your esteem, and I wish you not to forget me. With part of this, procure the liberty of your Mella; and may the rest add to the comforts of your age."

"Forget you!" repeated Carlo emphatically. "Never, Sir Henry! You were the first who spoke peace to my wounded spirit.—Yes, from this I will indeed redeem my Mella; and her presence shall prove a perpetual memento of your friendship. A few hours, Sir Henry, and I shall behold you no more: here, then, take an old man's blessing; and may you experience happiness equal to that you have conferred on me!"

Sir Henry shook his hand, and Carlo, sinking on his knee, pressed that of his youthful benefactor to his bosom and his lips, and, repeating his blessing, hastily withdrew. Sir Henry then returned to the Captain; who soon after took his final leave of the amiable Marchioness and the Governor.

The next morning Sir Henry and Frederick attended to conduct Harland and his bride on board. The painful moment of separation was arrived: the Marchioness and her daughters endeavoured to appear cheerful and collected; but the respectful and affectionate behaviour of Louise had too much endeared her to them to permit them to part without regret; nor could the obtrusive tear be restrained.

"We may meet again, my dear girl!" said the Marchioness, as the signal-gun warned them to depart. Harland gently forced his Louise from the arms of her early friends, and, placing her in the barge, they were soon conveyed on board. The signal was given to weigh—Louise faintly murmured the name of her benefactress; who with her daughters still sighed a blessing and adieu, as the unfurled sails swelled with the breeze which conveyed them from the romantic cliffs of St. Helena.

CHAPTER III.

The mind of Harland now enjoyed a serenity hitherto unknown; the mildness of Louise, the increasing knowledge of her virtues, whilst they added to his love, softened the harshness of his manners: and, from experiencing the sweets arising from beneficence, he was taught to regard the happiness of others, as conducive to his own.

It was one of those evenings when the serenity of the heavens shed its influence on mankind, and harmonized the mind to happiness, that the Captain, with his youthful companions, after long enjoying the tranquil beauties of the declining day, retired to his cabin. The careful mariner, freed for a time from toil, reclined in easy repose on the deck, or carrolled his humble ditty, as he watched the different vessels, of which he might be deemed in part the safeguard. A transient peace possessed every bosom: when Harland, after a considerable pause, addressing his Louise, said—"I have often designed, my dear girl, to request some account of the occurrences attending your childhood; of which I have hitherto had a very imperfect knowledge: the present moment is favourable for the relation, which I think would prove equally gratifying to Sir Henry and our friends."

"There is not any thing in the account, Harland," replied Louise, "to repay your attention in the hearing: a monastic life affords but little variety."— However, as Sir Henry and Frederick joined in the request, she without farther hesitation complied.

"Of the manner in which I was left at the gate of the Convent, you have already, Harland, been informed. I was found there in the morning by the portress, and by her carried to the mother St. Claire, the venerable Abbess. The meanness of my clothes by no means accorded with the valuable miniature tied round my neck; but rather tended, as the worthy Abbess said, to show that my parents were actuated by shame, not poverty. She, however, hesitated not a moment to take me in, and, after an ineffectual search to discover the authors of my being, determined to rear me, and dedicate my life me to the God who had placed me under her protection.

"I was accordingly given to the care of a lay sister, who faithfully discharged her trust; and as my infant mind expanded, the Abbess became each day more partial to me. The friendship of the mother St. Claire was followed by the real or pretended love of the other inmates of the Convent, and I was soon the avowed favourite of all.

"Amongst those, however, who evinced a sincere regard for me, was the sister Françoise; between whom, and the venerable Abbess, my early affection was divided. Under their more immediate care, I was instructed in every useful and ornamental branch of education; and their approbation and praise were the rewards of my diligence. Thus passed my earlier days, unclouded with a sorrow; sister Françoise and the Abbess were all the world to me, nor knew I of one beyond the walls of the Convent.

"The frequent visits, however, paid to the other children by their friends, could not but lead me, at length, to reflect on the difference of my lot. No father, no mother, ever inquired for me; and the first sigh that ever swelled my bosom, was for those relations, whom fate prohibited me from ever knowing."

A half-stifled sigh escaped Sir Henry; which was gently returned by Louise, who, after a moment's pause, again proceeded.

"Sister Françoise soon observed, and learned the cause of my dejection. 'You have no acknowledged parents, Louise,' she said; 'but I will be your mother, and you shall love me as a daughter.' She burst into tears; I kissed them off her cheek as she embraced me, and, pleased with the idea of mother, soon regained my cheerfulness. From that time, I became the nearly inseparable companion of sister Françoise: I addressed her by the name of mother, I believed her such, and fully did her tenderness authorise the title.

"It was not till I was fourteen, that mother St. Claire put into my possession the miniature found with me, and informed me of the circumstance which had placed me under her protection, and of her intentions that I should take the veil. The latter intelligence, repugnant as it was to my inclinations, affected me less than the knowledge of my orphan state. 'And is not sister Françoise then my mother?' I would have asked; but tears impeded my utterance; and, throwing my arms round the neck of St. Claire, I wept in silence. She tenderly embraced me; and when the violence of my grief was abated, exhorted me to resignation to the state that Providence had assigned me; and explained the reasons which rendered a life of seclusion necessary to one, who without friends could only look for infamy and destruction in the world.

"'Yet do not, dear mother,' I exclaimed, 'force me to be a nun—at least, not yet!'

"'Force you, my child!' repeated the venerable woman, 'never! Forced vows cannot be sincere; and sincere indeed ought those to be, which are offered to your God! You yet are young: but two years hence, if I be in existence, I hope to receive you at the altar. I have pointed out the dangers which would attend you, in a world you are a stranger to; you know the peaceful happiness, the security which reign within these walls: let both be the subject of your reflections; and too well am I assured of the sense, the goodness of heart my girl possesses, to doubt her cheerful acquiescence in the lot assigned her."

"Never before had my heart refused accordance to the sentiments or wishes of this my earliest friend; but the fascinating picture, the young Victoire, and Julie de Valois, (for three years my intimate companions) had often painted of the world, had first engaged my attention by its novelty, then taught me to wish for those pleasures, with which I thought it abounded. The world,—however, its gaieties—all were absorbed in the circumstance of my deserted infancy; and I left the worthy Abbess, overwhelmed with the only real sorrow I had ever known.

"Instead of going to my beloved mother, as I had hitherto termed her, I sought the gloomy solitude of the cloister; and was indulging in an unrestrained flow of tears, when the approach of two nuns caused me to retreat into an adjoining chapel. They seated themselves at the entrance, nor could I then have re-passed without discovery; which would have exposed me to a severe reproof from sister Brigide (one of them), for my intrusion into a place, sacred to the sisterhood. They, however, continued their discourse without the slightest suspicion of unhallowed ears, and I soon found sister Françoise was the subject of their conversation.

"'I, who have been an inmate here these six-and-thirty years,' said sister Brigide, 'am less regarded by the superannuated mother St. Claire; I may, however, one day be head of this convent; then woe betide some, whom I shall not name.'

"'How long is it since she took the veil?' asked the other, whom, by her voice I discovered to be a sister lately professed. 'Fourteen years,' answered Brigide: 'just after the Abbess's favourite Louise was left here; and much I mistake, if Françoise be not really her mother!'

"'Her great partiality to the child,' answered sister Marie, 'may certainly justify the suspicion.'

"'Suspicion'—repeated Brigide; 'I have proofs—facts, indubitable ones! I know more of sister Françoise than she thinks.'

"The curiosity of Marie thus raised, induced her to press Brigide to an explanation; whilst I scarcely respired lest a syllable of the important intelligence should escape me.

"'It is now about fifteen years,' said Brigide, 'since sister Françoise, then Mademoiselle de Colline, was a reigning belle; though, for my part, I never could discover the surprising beauty they say she possessed: being, however, the youngest daughter, she was designed for a monastic life; but was by nature more inclined to vows of love than religion. By her artful coquetries she at last fascinated a young Englishman who was on his travels, and who demanded her of her father in marriage. Monsieur de Colline refused him, he being an heretic; and the gallant apparently ceased his addresses; but after a lapse of some time, he was detected one morning by her father, descending from her chamber window. Justly enraged at the depravity of his daughter and the young fellow, Monsieur de Colline seized his pistols, and as the lover was scaling the garden-wall, a brace of bullets brought him to the earth!

"'Not satisfied with this victim to his injured honour, he hastened to the apartment of his daughter, taxed her with her crime, and was proceeding to tell her the vengeance he had taken, when the guilty wretch fell into fits, and was discovered to be in a state of pregnancy!

"'Her sisters, who before had been inclined to pity her, then abandoned her to the fury of her father; and happy had it been, if she had then expiated her sin by the loss of life; but an old servant, who had been privy to her amour, preserved her from the effects of his passion. She was, however, by his order, confined in an obscure part of the Chateau, and treated with the greatest rigour; but, instead of bewailing her fault, she only deplored the loss of her lover! There, with the assistance of her old confidant, she was delivered of an infant: its sex I never learned, or what became of it; but about that time Louise was found at the gates of the convent!'

"'Oh, a clear case—a clear case!' exclaimed sister Marie. 'But, with all the search they say St. Claire caused to be made for the parents, do not you think it strange these circumstances did not lead her to them?'

"'Not at all,' replied Brigide. 'The events I have related were transacted in too secret a manner to let suspicion even point a finger at the De Collines; nor do I believe there is another in the Convent, except the Abbess, who is acquainted with these particulars respecting her; nor should I have known them, but for the old confidant I mentioned; who, about five years since, became a lay sister, and died here. She too was very fond of Louise: and a few words she one day inadvertently uttered, raised my suspicion there was more concerning sister Françoise than I knew; and I determined never to rest till I had discovered what it was; and by a thousand questions, and indeed by pretending I was in the confidence of Françoise, I learned what I have now related.'—

"Sufficient indeed," interrupted Sir Henry, starting from his seat, and pacing the cabin, "to blast her character; but not to draw the tear of pity, the unhappy—injured Françoise deserved! Not even a convent, I find, can screen the unfortunate from malice and detraction!—But proceed, my dear Louise; I meant not to interrupt you."

"And did you, my brother," asked Louise, "ever before hear the misfortunes of Françoise?"

"I learned them from herself, Louise."

"From herself, Sir Henry! When did you know her?"

"Not till after you, my sister, left the convent. And here let me endeavour to do justice to her character. To the lover sister Brigide mentioned, Françoise, on her father's refusal, was privately united: and, by the assistance of the old servant, who witnessed their marriage, he was secretly admitted into the house. This intercourse had continued several months, when her father saw, and shot the unhappy husband; who was soon after found nearly lifeless, by some peasants, and by them conveyed to the house of a surgeon.

"In Monsieur de Colline's subsequent interview with Françoise, she avowed her marriage; but he either did not—or would not believe her. He caused her to be confined, and fearing, if she persisted in her declaration of marriage, he could not force her to take the veil; he not only informed her, her lover was dead, but, to further his purpose, that her infant likewise expired soon after its birth. By him it was indeed doomed to expiate, by its death, the supposed fault of its wretched mother: but Providence preserved it for a better fate.

"Françoise, however—her heart nearly broken by the double loss of her husband and child—gladly availed herself of the fate designed her, to escape the reproaches of her father, and the taunts of her sisters, and threw herself into the convent of St. Ursule; where she took the veil at the very time her husband, recovered of his wound, was searching the country to discover her: but Monsieur de Colline had taken his measures too effectually; and at last, supposing her dead, he returned to England. At the old man's death, however, the letters the unhappy Henry had addressed to Françoise, and to him, were discovered by his Confessor; as likewise the Monk who had married them; and as her husband was then living, a dispensation was obtained, and sister Françoise, freed from her vows, returned with my father to England."

"Your father! O God, my brother!" exclaimed Louise, clasping her hands. "Tell me, I entreat you, if Françoise de Colline was really my mother!"

Sir Henry appeared confused—distressed: but at last said—"Seek not, my dear girl, the knowledge which cannot add to your happiness, but would plunge me still deeper in the gulf of misery. Your mother lives: and you shall one day know her. The time, alas! will too soon arrive, when every midnight deed must be brought to light: but, till then—let not the hand of Louise level an unnecessary shaft at my bosom!"

Louise could urge no farther; her anxiety to be satisfied on this subject, yielded to the visible concern and agitation her question had occasioned Sir Henry. She sighed, and a pause ensued, from which they were relieved by the Captain requesting her to proceed in her narrative.

"Little more passed," continued Louise, "between sister Brigide and Marie, than what I have related. The latter mentioned the miniature found with me, as a proof that must instantly confirm the truth of Brigide's allegation; but Brigide ridiculed the idea. She had seen the miniature, she said, it was not of Françoise: but Monsieur de Colline and his daughter were both too cunning, she added, to leave any proof with me, which must discover them; the miniature was a trinket, by which if ever they chose to reclaim me, they could; but a ring or a seal would have answered the purpose equally the same.—They were here interrupted by the arrival of another nun, with whom they proceeded to the refectory; whilst I, freed from the danger of detection, hastened to the cell of sister Françoise, and, throwing myself into her arms, exclaimed—'I am—I am your child; oh, do not attempt to deceive me, but say that you are indeed my mother!'

"Sister Françoise was at first alarmed at the wildness of my address, but, on my relating the discoveries of the morning, her agitation far exceeded my own.—'No—no, Louise,' she sighed, 'you are not my child: would to heaven that you were: but I am indeed widowed—and childless!'

"She wrung her hands, and, bursting into tears, sunk on her humble couch. I mingled my tears with hers; I strove to soothe her; yet still urged my claim to maternal acknowledgment. She referred me to the miniature:—'The resemblance you bear to it, Louise,' she said, 'must convince you it was done for a parent; but no likeness can be traced in it to me. Cease then to wring my soul by forcing to remembrance, scenes long since passed. I love you, Louise; but utterly disclaim all kindred with your blood. Be satisfied then with my affection, nor ever again renew this subject to me or any one!'

"Thus prohibited, I forbore to speak, but sighed in secret over the mystery of my birth; my mind by degrees lost its serenity, and I was apprehended to be in a decline; when the Marchioness de Valois came to the Convent. The friendship of her lovely daughters had before introduced me to her notice; she regarded me with an eye of pity, and proposed my going with her to Montpellier. The worthy St. Claire readily consented; and taking an affectionate leave of her and sister Françoise, for the first time in my life, I re-passed the gates of the Convent.

"What were my sentiments of the various objects I beheld, I shall leave to your own conceptions; all indeed was wonder, joy, and amazement! The amiable Marchioness, pleased with my inquiries and remarks, pointed out and explained whatever she thought worthy my notice or regard. She did more: she traced the grief which oppressed me to its source, and wiped the tear of dejection from my cheek. She taught me to look forward with hope, and to rely with confidence on the wisdom of Providence, which, in its own time, would develope the mystery that distressed me. The friendship of this amiable woman, the paternal behaviour of the Marquis, who joined us at Montpellier, and the amusements of that celebrated place, to me so novel, soon restored my wonted cheerfulness and health; and, after an absence of three months, I returned to the Convent; where the increased infirmities of mother St. Claire, and a fever with which sister Françoise was seized, called forth all my tenderness and attention.

"They were repaid by the restoration of this mother of my affection, and the mild serenity of the venerable Abbess; who, unalarmed, awaited the hour of dissolution, with a smile of confidence and peace, that anticipated the reward of a life passed in piety and benevolence. Her fondness for me appeared daily to increase; but, to my great surprise and satisfaction, she no longer urged my taking the vows, or even expressed a wish for my engaging in a monastic life.

"Thus passed a twelvemonth, happy as those I had formerly known; when the Marchioness again came to the Convent, to take Victoire and Julie finally from under the care of St. Claire.

"It was then that she declared her intentions in my favour; to which St. Claire added—'For this reason, my child, I have long ceased importuning you to enter on your probation. You dislike the life of a nun, and, how much soever I wish for your society, I prefer your happiness and real advantage to my own gratification. Here you would be secure from the storms and cares of life; but, from what I have learned respecting sister Brigide, who will undoubtedly be my successor, you could hope for nothing more, save the peace arising from internal religion; and even that, the mother of a sisterhood has it in her power to disturb, though not to destroy. With me, you might experience the happiness a life of religion is calculated to afford; but see, my child,' and she turned a glass whose last sands were running out, 'my hour is nearly expired! To the Marchioness then I resign you.—Let the religion, the precepts I have inculcated, the example I have given you, prove the guides of your conduct.—Transfer the obedience you have shown me, to her; and may every happiness attend you!'

"Tears of affection and gratitude were my only answer; I could not speak, but, sinking at her feet, hid my face on her knees; the world I had sighed for, faded on my imagination before this instance of her love; and the thoughts of leaving her far outweighed the life of liberty she had awarded me.

"Orders, however, were given for my departure; nor did St. Claire provide for me as the orphan of her charity, but as the child of her tenderest regard. To the former marks of her munificence, she added many valuable presents. 'They will remind you of my lessons, Louise,' she said, 'even in the assemblies of the gay. I shall feel the loss of your attentions, but sister Françoise will supply your place; and remember, my child, whilst I have life, you shall be welcomed here with open arms!'

"All was soon prepared, and receiving her final blessing, with that of sister Françoise, I followed the Marchioness to her carriage.

"We proceeded to Paris, where a continued round of amusements for some time banished reflection, and the remembrance of the worthy St. Claire. Pleasure, however, at length lost its attractions, and only in the friendship of the Marchioness, and a few select families, I found that real satisfaction I had in vain expected in the more brilliant, but dissipated circles of the fashionable world.

"Twelve months had elapsed, since I quitted the Convent; I had repeatedly written to St. Claire and sister Françoise, but never received an answer: and as we were then going to the Marquis's country seat, the Marchioness consented that I should cross the country to Rennes. It was late in the evening when I arrived at the Convent; painfully anticipating the intelligence of St. Claire's death: there, instead of the benevolent mild old sister Marthe, who first succoured my helpless infancy, a lay sister I had never seen, attended the summons to the gate, and demanded my business?

"'Is mother St. Claire still living?' I tremulously asked.

"'She has been dead eleven months,' replied the portress; 'and mother St. Brigide is now the head of this Convent. If you wish to speak with her, send in your name and business, and I will endeavour to gain you admittance.'

"'Oh no,' I exclaimed—'not with her: but tell sister Françoise, her child—her Louise, wishes to see her.'

"'Louise—sister Françoise!' she repeated with a frown. 'There is no such sister within these walls.'

"'O God!' I cried. 'Is she too dead?'

"'I have positive orders,' said the portress, 'not to answer any questions, or take in any message from you.'—She closed the grate: and Jacques hearing what passed, of his own accord drove to an hotel, where I passed the night in mournful reflections, and the next day, with an oppressed heart, rejoined the Marchioness at Rohan.

"No occurrence happened from that time, till nearly a twelvemonth after, when the Count de Dreux declared himself my admirer. He was nearly fifty—vain, self-sufficient, and affected; but likewise rich; and, for the last consideration, the Marquis advised my encouragement of his addresses: to the Marchioness, however, I avowed my real sentiments respecting him; and she gave him a gentle, but positive refusal. At the same time she undeceived him respecting my birth, by which he had supposed me nearly related to her; and that consideration, I believe, reconciled him to her rejection; but though he ceased to regard me as longer worthy his honourable addresses, he still pursued me, as an object of desire.

"At that time the Marquis was unexpectedly appointed Governor of Pondicherry; for which place he was ordered immediately to depart.

"The Marchioness accompanied him to L'Orient, whither I should likewise have attended her with Victoire and Julie, but indisposition obliged me to remain at the Chateau. The opportunity was too favourable to the projects of the Count, to be neglected; he wrote me a passionate letter, with a brilliant offer of settlements, jewels, &c.: of which I did not deign to take the least notice. My silence produced a second, on the supposition that he had not been sufficiently liberal: and he sent a carte blanche. To evince my contempt, I tore the letters, and returned them in a cover; and, as I was surrounded by faithful servants, and two days elapsed without hearing of him, I apprehended no farther molestation or danger.

"On the morning of the third, however, a courier, covered with dust, and apparently fatigued, arrived at the Chateau. He came, he said, from L'Orient, where the Marchioness, who had been overturned in her carriage, was in the most imminent danger. He brought a letter, as he pretended, from her femme-de-chambre, which repeated the information, and begged my immediate presence, as Victoire and Julie were in the greatest affliction.

"Alarmed at this account of my beloved benefactress, I gave orders for a chaise to be instantly prepared; and, without an idea occurring that the tale might be fictitious, assisted my maid to pack up a change of apparel. The chaise was soon ready, and I set out for L'Orient, attended by Janette, the false courier, and two old servants, who, on hearing the accident which had happened, entreated they might accompany me. We proceeded with great expedition, and were within a few miles of L'Orient, when, on passing a thicket, two men on horseback suddenly approached; one stopped the horses, whilst the other, presenting a pistol to Jacques, threatened to shoot him if he offered to proceed. The faithful Grégoire, perceiving the situation of his fellow-servant, would have advanced to his assistance, but was withheld by the pretended messenger; who seized him by the collar, and a scuffle immediately ensued. A carriage then approached, from which the Count himself alighted; and, opening the door of my chaise, he attempted to force me out. Vain would have been my resistance, had not a sailor, attracted I believe by my screams, darted from the thicket, and with a bludgeon struck the Count to the ground.

"What directly followed, I cannot say, as I fainted; but, as Janette afterwards informed me, the men who first stopped us, seeing their master fall, sprung to defend him, and old Jacques finding himself at liberty, without regarding the sailor who had so gallantly come to our assistance, or Grégoire, drove off with the utmost velocity.—When I recovered, we were far from the scene of contention; and as Jacques, equally alarmed as myself, still urged the speed of his horses, we soon arrived at L'Orient.

"I found my beloved benefactress well, but dejected from the departure of the Marquis, who had sailed the day before. On relating my tale, she expressed her satisfaction at my escape from the Count; and, convinced the greatest care was necessary to guard me from his machinations, determined in future not to trust me from her own immediate protection.

"Soon after this, Grégoire arrived, and informed us that the men who first stopped us, prepared to pursue me; but were remanded by the valet, on the supposition that the Count was dead.—After some time, however, he showed signs of returning life and sense, and whilst they were replacing him in his carriage, to re-convey him to a seat he possessed near the spot, (whither he had proposed to carry me), the sailor, who had at first been secured, made his escape again into the thicket. As for Grégoire, he was no longer regarded either in a hostile or amicable manner, and accordingly remounted his horse, and followed us to L'Orient.

"The next day we returned to the Chateau, at which place the Marchioness proposed remaining, till the vessel preparing to take the family, should be ready to sail. A month of tranquillity ensued, when we were surprised by a visit from the Count. The obstacles he had met with, it appeared, so far from abating, had added to his desire of obtaining me; but, convinced of the impracticability of either seducing, or forcing me from the protection of the Marchioness, and being, he said, unable to exist without me, he again demanded my hand in marriage. The Marchioness would have urged my accedence to an establishment so brilliant; but, on declaring my utter dislike to him, she yielded, and again gave him a positive refusal.

"The Count, mortified and enraged at my repeated rejections, vowed never to quit the pursuit, till he had, either by honourable or other means, subdued my obduracy. Secure, however, in the friendship of the Marchioness, I equally disregarded his entreaties and threats; and the vessel appointed for us, being fully prepared, and the fleet ready to sail, we bade adieu to France; and I was thus happily freed from the importunities of a troublesome lover."

"Thanks, my dear Louise," said Harland, "for your interesting tale; which, though unmarked with any extraordinary occurrences, proves you to have been truly the child of Providence."

"The child of Providence indeed," repeated Sir Henry, "nor can I sufficiently admire the wisdom of that Power, who directs the most trivial of our actions.

Little did I think, when I hastened to your rescue, it was to that of the sister, of whom I was then in search. Your fainting, and the confusion arising from the unlucky blow I gave the Count, prevented me from observing you; and on that nobleman's partial recovery, I was glad to elude the vigilance of his servants, and seek the shelter the luxurious foliage of the thicket afforded."

"And was it you, my brother," said Louise, in a voice of grateful mildness, "who then preserved me from the Count? But what accident conducted you to so solitary a spot? and why in a garb so unsuitable to your station and character?"

"Mrs. Harland has anticipated the question, I was in part going to ask Sir Henry," said the Captain; "and as you have raised my curiosity, if you will acquaint us with the particulars of your peregrination in France, which you mentioned when at St. Helena, it will add to the pleasure I have received in hearing the relation of your sister?"

Sir Henry readily complied—"although I have little to recite," he said, "except an action I must ever remember with regret, as a weakness for which one so long inured to sorrow as myself, can offer no excuse."

CHAPTER IV.

"When at St. Helena, I believe I informed you I went from Cardigan to Havre-de-Grace, as a common sailor; I there determined to seek a sister, endeared to me by misfortune as well as the ties of blood; and accordingly directed my steps to Rennes; my whole wealth consisting in the clothes I wore, which were those I obtained by exchange from a lad near Harwich, and the wages arising from my voyage. This little stock, however, was insufficient to bear my expenses, and the last day I travelled without money or food; but hope impelled me forward, and on my arrival at Rennes, I inquired my way to the Convent of St. Ursule. My appearance there was too mean to gain me access to the Abbess, or even procure me a civil answer to the question I asked, whether Louise were living, and residing in the Convent? The portress disclaimed all knowledge of the circumstance—or the child I alluded to, and finally closed the grate to my face.

"Thus repulsed, I slowly turned from the gate, and directed my steps to an humble *auberge*, where I threw myself on a bench in the yard, in a state of mind painfully depressed. The hope I had indulged to a most sanguine degree of finding Louise, and being acknowledged by her as a brother, and which had cheered me on my journey, and soothed me in my moments of sadness, was thus completely destroyed; nor had I then the least clue to guide me to her.

"Was my sister dead? I asked myself—or had I been deceived?

"The question led to events long since past; busy memory, in vivid colours, brought to view each circumstance which had progressively involved me in a state of wretchedness, and made me feel with maddening exaggeration a fate I thought unmerited. I was indeed driven by a power I could not oppose, from kindred, friends, and fortune—a wanderer on a foreign shore, without even the means of procuring a single meal to satisfy the wants of nature.— The only prospect before me, was beggary!

"The idea was too much—my passions, long restrained, with a violence not to be controlled, o'erburst the bounds of reason; franticly I called for death; cursed the hour that gave me to the arms of my parents; and bade the earth open and bury me for ever in her bosom!

"What inconsistencies I was guilty of, I cannot say; I was unconscious of observation—of all around me!—and such ascendancy did my madness at last attain, that I thought I heard the voice of my father in the breeze, chiding me for living in a world, where I had lost every prospect of happiness.

"The conceit led to self-destruction; and suicide instantly presented itself to my fevered imagination, as affording the oblivion I coveted. Wildly my eye glanced to every object, in search of some instrument wherewith to perpetrate my design; but none presented itself. A well, however, met my view, and, starting from my seat, I ran with an intention of precipitating myself into it. Already had I reached the brink, when my arm was arrested, with a violence, which not only prevented my design, but forced me some paces back from the place of destruction.

"The shock in some degree recalled my recollection, and, raising my eyes, I beheld an old *religieux*, to whose timely interposition I was indebted for preservation. The tear started to his eye, and his right hand trembled as he grasped my arm; he gently raised his other toward heaven, and regarded me with such a look, as struck me to the the heart; and reproved me more forcibly, than language could have done, for my temerity in daring to rush unsummoned into the presence of my Maker!

"The tempest of my mind ceased; but was succeeded by a horror and remorse, I cannot attempt to describe. I passively permitted the worthy Monk to conduct me to the seat I had quitted; where, placing himself beside me, he hesitatingly asked, what had induced me to attempt self-destruction?

"I would have offered an extenuation of my madness; but my words were incoherent. He stopped me—'Suicide, my son, can admit of no excuse!—Misfortune and sorrow attend us all, from the monarch to the lowest mendicant; but, were the burden ten times heavier than that inflicted, it is our duty to bear it! I saw you in the street; your appearance bespoke distress, and I followed, for the purpose of affording that relief, I thought you merited. The action I have witnessed here, young man,' he continued with severity, 'I need not comment on; your own conscience, I trust, will sufficiently speak its enormity.'

"I could not look up—I dared not meet his penetrating eye: and shame added an additional pang to sorrow.—He saw the struggle in my bosom, and pity regained her influence: his voice softened—'Forgive my harshness, youth; I ought perhaps rather to apply the balm of consolation to a mind diseased, than by reproaches add to its malady: but you appear faint, my child;—perhaps for want of sustenance?'—He anxiously arose, and beckoning the host, desired him to carry some wine and provisions into a private room; then again addressing me, proffered his assistance to conduct me into the house.

"A false pride at first made me recoil: but the benevolence which beamed in his eyes, as he gently drew my hand on his arm, checked the ungrateful sentiment.

"I attended him to a room, where the humble Jean officiously spread a table with the little dainties of the larder; but a significant glance from my entertainer telling him his presence could be dispensed with, he respectfully bowed and retired. The worthy Monk then pressed me to eat; filled a glass with wine, and placed it near my plate: but all was ineffectual; my mind, more exhausted than my body, required that support he vainly offered to my enfeebled frame. I would in gratitude have eaten, but nature refused her office. He looked grieved—'Your sorrows, my son, I believe, are deeper than I at first imagined. Your looks—your deportment, bespeak you acquainted with fairer scenes in life, as well as with misfortune. Tell me—am I mistaken?'

"'You are not, Father,' I replied, 'and the action you lately witnessed, may tell you those misfortunes are neither trivial nor common. I am indeed the child of misery!'

"'Alas! my son,' he returned with a sigh, 'we view the events of life through the glass of prejudice. When misfortunes oppress us, we look through the magnifying end, and think our own afflictions by far the most superior: and, by the same rule, we reverse the glass to the distresses of others, and see them in a lessened point of view: still judging the happiness or misery of the world by our own feelings. Yet, true it is, that which afflicts you, might by another be disregarded; and that which would bow another to the grave, you, perhaps, could support with fortitude! It is the hand of a Power, which cannot err, that dispenses our portion of good and evil to each according to his abilities of bearing. Take religion for your staff, my son, and integrity for your guide, and the misfortunes of the world combined, can never crush you!'

"'Ah! Father,' I cried, 'resignation is easy in theory, to those who have only to preach it. Sheltered yourself from misfortune, how can you judge of that, which drove me a fugitive from hope and happiness?'

"'I can judge,' said he solemnly; 'for I have experienced sorrow; and I preach—from my practice! Listen to my tale, young man, with attention, and from my misfortunes learn to bear your own without repining.—

"'Monsieur La Roche, my father, was in his youth clerk to a merchant at Nantes, and early in life married a woman in circumstances humble as his own. I was the only fruit of that marriage, my mother dying of a decline, a few months after my birth. My father, however, did not long remain in a state of widowhood; for the only daughter of his master, who had long entertained a partiality for him, inadvertently so far discovered her sentiments, that he was emboldened to offer secret addresses; and a private marriage soon after made him the presumptive heir to his master. The old gentleman, who certainly had expected a more suitable match for his daughter, was yet too doatingly fond of her, to refuse the forgiveness she entreated: and the respectful behaviour of my father to him, and his strict application to business, in a little time, not only reconciled him to her imprudent choice, but raised my father so high in his esteem, that he voluntarily took him into partnership.

"'By my mother-in-law, who had not any children, and this worthy man, I was ever treated with the greatest tenderness, but in less than five years, a malignant fever broke out at Nantes, and, amongst its numerous victims, carried the gentle Madeleine and her sire to the grave; leaving my father, for the second time, what the world called, an inconsolable widower. He found himself, however, master of a princely fortune; and, in less than twelve months, surprised the world, by a third marriage—and that with the femme-de-chambre of his late wife!

"'From that period I date the commencement of the sorrows and misfortunes which attended me, till my head was silvered by the hand of time!

"'Madame La Roche, my new mother-in-law, who far exceeded her predecessors in personal attractions, soon gained a complete ascendancy over my father: and as, in the course of three years, she presented him with as many children, she began to regard me with an eye of jealous hatred. This showed itself on a variety of occasions, and one day, on my father honouring me with his notice, a thing rather unusual, she peremptorily insisted on my being sent to a public academy. My father yielded, and I was thus banished from home—never to be recalled!

"'At first I rejoiced at being freed from the tyranny of Madame La Roche; but after passing three years, without once visiting the habitation of my father, I began to think my lot peculiarly hard; till the master informed me I was not to return till my education was completed. This reason satisfied me, and three years more elapsed, when I was surprised by a visit from Monsieur and Madame La Roche. My father beheld me without emotion, and, on his wife declaring that my uncouth appearance would disgrace the family, readily agreed to her proposal of binding me apprentice to some reputable tradesman. I timidly expressed my wish of being placed in his counting-house, but was refused by Madame with a frown; and after telling me I must remain at the academy till they had fixed on a trade suitable to my genius, they departed.

"'About three weeks after, a chaise was sent for me, in which I was conveyed to the house of a printer, in the suburbs of Nantes, where I was immediately settled as an apprentice for seven years.

"'There I endured every mortification, ill nature and arrogance could inflict; heightened by the comparison of my lot to those of my brothers, whom I frequently saw, with their mother, in all the pomp of dress and equipage!

"'Slowly passed the time in my imagination, till I had completed the term of my servitude: still had I indulged hopes that my father would receive me into his house, if not as a son, at least as an assistant; when I determined, by the most circumspect behaviour, to obliterate, if possible, the unfavourable sentiments he entertained of me. But vain were my hopes; my mother-in-law's influence overbalanced the weak claim I had to his regard. When I went to his house, he was not at home, the servant said, and I was refused admittance. I again went, and was rudely reprimanded by the menial for being troublesome. I then wrote to my father, urged my claim of nature, to his notice and protection, and appealed to his heart, if any part of my conduct had given just cause for the neglect with which I had been treated? I coveted not his wealth, I said, but to his affection I felt I had an equal claim with his other children.

"'This letter was answered by Madame La Roche. She coolly denied the justness of my claim, by reminding me I had never been regarded as one of the family: however, as she acknowledged I had some small demand on their notice, she remitted me a draft for two thousand livres; a sum sufficient, she said, to establish me respectably: and to my own diligence I must look for future supplies. My father added a postscript, to confirm the decree of his wife, and advised my proceeding to Paris, as a place where industry was most likely to be rewarded.

"'A tear of wounded sensibility forced its way down my cheek, at this final act and renunciation of my father: I, however, determined to show my obedience to his will, cruel as it was, and, accordingly, a few days after receiving my small fortune, set out for Paris, having been previously refused the liberty of writing to him.

"'On my arrival at Paris, I determined to engage as a journeyman to some master, till I should meet with a situation to my satisfaction; and not, by plunging into business without friends or connexions, with so small a principal, hazard what might terminate in my ruin.

"'With a printer in the Fauxbourg St. Germain, I engaged, and passed three years in that humble station, when I married an amiable woman, who declared herself willing to share the frowns or smiles of fortune with me; and for two years experienced a happiness interrupted only by the remembrance of my father.

"'A smiling infant crowned our love. Fortune, too, assumed a fairer aspect. My master retired from business; and, though it required a larger capital than I possessed, I ventured to take it, relying on my own application to clear the debt I incurred.

"'But, alas! weak man!—I read not the volume of my fate: I dreaded not the wretchedness which in that hour of fancied prosperity awaited me!

"'Cheerfully I paid my little fortune into the hands of my master, and gave him my bond for the residue of the debt. But scarcely had we been settled in our new habitation a week, when, in the night, I was roused from a peaceful slumber by the alarm of fire! I instantly awoke my wife, and, starting from the bed, ran to the staircase,—but, alas! it was in flames! I then hastened to the window, and called for assistance, but its situation was too obscure to gain me notice; and my voice was unheard amidst the noise and confusion which reigned in the street, where all were assiduous to assist and save an opulent family, whose house adjoined mine, and where the fire, I believe, originally began. In this distressing situation, we remained, nearly suffocated with smoke, till the flames began to appear through the floor of the room:—not another moment, I found, was to be lost:—I clasped my infant daughter to my bosom, and, springing on the frame of the window, bade my wife trust herself to my arms, and, by throwing ourselves into the street, either be saved or perish together! She approached—the height appalled her—she drew back—hesitated—the floor gave way, and she sunk to a grave—horrid as inevitable!

"'The flames raged around me with the maddest fury, and, unable to withstand their force, I gave a groan of anguish to the fate of my wretched wife, and threw myself from the window. I fell unnoticed: two of my ribs and my arm were broken, and my hapless infant killed on the spot: but oblivion drew her veil over my senses, and for some hours kindly saved me from the knowledge of my misery. I was at last discovered; and, as I was afterwards informed, carried to several houses in the neighbourhood, but no one had charity sufficient to receive me. I was therefore conveyed to an hospital, where proper means were used for my restoration; but the last shriek of my wife still vibrated in my ears: her last look, with all its horrors, still pierced my heart: the innocent pressure of my infant to my bosom—all combined to tear reason from her seat. My fractures were healed, and I was removed from the hospital to a madhouse.'

"The worthy Monk," said Sir Henry, "here paused, whilst a tear unbidden forced its way from his eye. I attempted not to speak: my faculties, indeed, were suspended by his tale; and I still regarded him with a look of silent attention, sufficiently expressive, I believe, of the commiseration and curiosity I felt, and which had, for the time, wholly banished my own afflictions from my mind.

"His voice soon regained its wonted tone, when he thus continued the relation of his misfortunes.

"'It was three years before my senses regained their usual tenour; when I was permitted to enter on the world to seek subsistence. The accidents I had met with, I thought might authorise an application to my father. I accordingly wrote; but he was dead, and his fortune wholly settled on my brothers and Madame La Roche! She condescended to inform me of these particulars, and testified her surprise at my application, after the liberal provision formerly bestowed on me, which, she said, if I had either squandered or lost, I must answer to myself, as she should by no means injure her fortune to re-establish mine.

"'I gave a tear to the memory of my father, which, however neglectful he had been of my welfare, I still held sacred. To my lot of poverty I submitted with feelings of mingled regret and resignation; and once more sought employment as a journeyman. But sorrow had robbed me of my vivacity; my mind had been deranged; some believed it so still; few cared to trust me; and fewer to employ, or pay me for my labour. At last, unable to bear the penury which threatened me, I left Paris: and, after unsuccessful applications for employ, in various places, I was received on moderate wages by a printer at St. Malo's. I there by degrees recovered my health and spirits, and served my master with such attention and diligence, that, at the end of five years, he agreed to admit me as a partner in his business, allowing me a small share of the profits, independently of my salary. Here then fortune once more began to smile, and for four years rewarded my assiduity with success.

"'At that time my master consented to take me into equal partnership; and I was on the point of marriage with a young lady of small fortune; when one evening, as I was returning home, I was accosted by a countrywoman with an infant, who earnestly entreated I would direct her the road to Rennes. I gave her the information she wanted, but observed it was too late for her to think of prosecuting her journey; and as she declared herself a stranger, offered to conduct her to a house of honest repute, where she might pass the night. She thanked me, and as she appeared much fatigued, I took the child in my arms and carried it. Some idle chat with the hostess and herself, when I had seen her accommodated to her satisfaction, detained me nearly an hour, when I returned home, little suspecting an action so trivial and innocent, would be the means of involving me again in trouble.

"'The next day, on visiting my intended bride, I was received with a reserve I could not account for; thinking, however, some occurrence, unconnected with me, might have occasioned a dissatisfaction as apparent as unusual, I concealed my observation of it; but, in the evening, on repeating my visit, her coldness had so far increased, that I could no longer refrain from asking an explanation: and was answered, by an accusation of an illicit connexion with the woman I had the preceding evening conducted to the auberge. My surprise at this unexpected charge, she construed into a confirmation of my guilt, and declared her resolution of instantly breaking off an acquaintance with a man, who had so wantonly deceived her. In vain I affirmed my innocence; related my accidental meeting with the woman, and appealed to her evidence for the truth of my assertion; but, with a look of reproachful triumph, as detecting my falsehood, she told me, the servant had seen me enter the auberge with my infant charge and its worthless mother; and on informing her, she herself went and questioned the woman concerning the nature of our acquaintance: and her answers, ambiguous as they were, were yet sufficient to condemn me. That she had at first declared herself a native of the place; then again, that she was a stranger, and unknown. That the child was hers—then, that she was only hired to take it from its mother.—Of its father, she would not give any account, but its likeness to me sufficiently proved that father to be myself! In vain I strove to reason—to rally her from an opinion so absurdly founded; she resented my justification, as an additional insult. Finding the foolish dispute likely to terminate too seriously, I at last insisted on the woman being sent for, and made to acknowledge to whom it was, the child belonged. Antoinette scornfully smiled at what she termed my artful subterfuge, as the woman, she said, had no doubt received her lesson. I could not conceal my vexation at this additional charge; but, however, sent for the peasant. She had left the town: I dispatched a person after her, on the road to Rennes: but her steps were not to be traced; and I remained stigmatised as an unprincipled debauchee, by the unjust suspicions of my mistress, and the tattling hostess.

"'Antoinette truly kept her word, in ceasing to admit of my addresses, and my master, to whom she was related, incensed at the breaking-off of the marriage, not only refused to fulfil his intentions in my favour, but dissolved our partnership, and dismissed me from his service!

"'At that time I entertained not the idea, but subsequent occurrences induce me to believe, that Antoinette was actuated by other motives than jealousy, for her conduct; as she soon after accepted the hand of a man, by far my junior, and in more affluent circumstances.

"'This, however, was but the commencement of my difficulties; for, whilst I was endeavouring to clear myself to my irritated master, a person inquired for me. On being admitted, he informed me, that Monsieur Orfévre, my former master in Paris, was dead; and that on examining his papers, a bond was found for two thousand livres, due from me, for the stock unfortunately consumed by fire. That his nephew, who succeeded to his property, understanding that I was in circumstances sufficiently affluent to discharge the obligation, had deputed him to receive the money.

"'The justness of the debt I attempted not to deny; yet, reflecting on the promise of the deceased, (which I declared), of expunging it, on account of my misfortune, I hesitated to pay the demand. The officer, for such he proved to be, coolly answered, if such had been the intentions of Monsieur Orfévre, he would undoubtedly have mentioned it in his will, or have destroyed the bond; and on my master saying I was capable of paying the debt, he immediately arrested me!

"'Thus compelled, I paid the money; which, by dint of the strictest frugality, I had accumulated, and found myself once more in the world, poor and friendless! I endeavoured to submit with patience to my lot; but injudiciously entered into business, without the means of pursuing it. This was regarded as an avowed opposition to my master, who highly resented the action; and as his interest and connexions were great, my exertions were rendered abortive. For two years I struggled for support—for bread; when my creditors finding me unable to satisfy their demands, completed my ruin by throwing me into prison.

"At first the gloomy horrors of the place, the misery of its inmates, deeply affected my mind, and each hour the sigh of sorrow swelled my bosom; till religion opened to my soul that source of comfort which can never fail; my prison lost its horrors, peace shed her gentlest influence on my slumbers, and marked my days with serenity: my brow lost its contraction, and my heart expanded, and bowed before the wisdom of my God! Contentedly I passed the day, in such work as the charity of a few individuals afforded me; by which means, I not only acquired sufficient to procure me what comforts my situation would admit of, but likewise to assist those more helpless than myself.

"'Thus passed fourteen years of my existence, when an English gentleman, actuated by curiosity, came to the prison. He saw—conversed with me; and at last inquired on what account I was confined? I told him, and the years I had been immured. He regarded me, as I spoke, with a look of the gentlest pity: the half-formed answer hung on his lips, but turning from me, he hastily left the prison.—In less than an hour, an order came for my enlargement! Scarcely could I credit the gaoler's assertion, that I was at liberty; yet, though weaned from the world, the thoughts of once more becoming an active member in it, made the tide of life, which had been wont to flow calmly through its channels, rush with reanimated force, and each pulse to beat with redoubled vigour. I raised my heart in thankfulness to God—I blessed the generous Corbet, and on the doors of the prison being opened to me, hastened to the hotel where he was. I was instantly shown to the room where he was sitting, with his lady; but such were my emotions, I could not return the thanks my heart dictated: I attempted to speak—and burst into tears! My benefactor instantly arose, and conducted me to a seat, and after pressing me to partake of refreshments, requested to be informed by what circumstances I had incurred the debt, for which I had so long suffered confinement. I instantly complied, and gave him a concise relation of my life: when I recounted my meeting with the peasant woman, the emotions of my auditors were too apparent to escape observation, and the words, 'Poor Louise!' faintly murmured by Sir Henry, (for so was my benefactor called), induce me to believe they were the parents of that infant.

"'Fearful of intruding, when I had concluded, I arose to depart; and Sir Henry, presenting me a small packet, said—'Oblige me, Monsieur La Roche, by accepting this trifle; little should I evince myself a friend, by leaving you exposed to indigence, or the fate from which I so lately rescued you. From the misfortunes you have experienced in your native land, you perhaps would feel little repugnance in quitting it; and I should advise you to seek a situation in the Eastern or Western settlements, where fortune yet may make you amends for your former losses.

"'Oppressed as I was by his late beneficence, I for a moment hesitated to receive this additional proof of his friendship, but the glance of his eye, beaming with benevolence, more than his words, urged my acceptance. I readily promised to follow his advice, and in language scarcely coherent, was endeavouring to express my gratitude, when the master of the packet came to inform them all was prepared for their departure for England. Sir Henry instantly arose, and presenting his hand to his fair companion, bade me a cordial and a last adieu. I followed at a humble distance, willing to retain a last view of a man I thought an honour to human nature. I saw them embark, and watched the vessel till they retired from the deck, when I slowly retraced my way into town. On examining the contents of my packet, I found in it, to the amount of a thousand crowns; a sum so far exceeding my expectation, I at first nearly doubted its reality: the sight of Antoinette and her husband, however, convinced me my senses retained their perfect powers; and as their appearance recalled ideas far from pleasing, I determined to quit St. Malo's that very evening. The few necessaries I wanted, were soon procured, and I set out towards L'Orient, intending to embark in some vessel for Madagascar or Pondicherry.

"'As I drew near L'Orient, however, I experienced a wish to take a last farewell of the place where I first drew breath; and therefore directed my steps to Nantes. I there visited every place I remembered as pleasing to my childhood; and having passed some hours greatly to my satisfaction, went to an hotel, where I inquired after my brothers, and my father's widow. Madame La Roche, the host informed me, had been dead some years, and her eldest son, to whom she left the principal part of her property, lived long enough to squander it, with that left him by my father, and died in consequence of his debaucheries. Her second son, a man of the fairest character and honour, and who had been brought up to the mercantile business, was lost about two years preceding my inquiry, in returning from America. The youngest, who had succeeded to his property, was the only one left of her descendants; and he had been thrown from his horse a few days before, and was so severely hurt, that the most serious apprehensions were entertained for his life.

"'I could not, unmoved, hear this account of my only relation; in that hour of affliction, I longed to claim the privilege of a brother; to minister to his wants, to speak the words of comfort, and soothe the anguish of a sick bed.—I at last determined to write: my advances might, perhaps, be rejected with disdain; but I should nevertheless, I thought, feel a satisfaction from the consciousness of having performed a duty. I accordingly wrote: but, contrary to my expectation, in less than an hour, my brother's chariot drove to the hotel, and the servants with the utmost obsequiousness, requested my presence immediately, at the house of their master. I went—and found my brother, as I expected, confined to his bed; a smile of satisfaction enlivened his manly features at my approach; for my resemblance to my father convinced him I was not an impostor. He immediately ordered his servants to pay the same deference to me, as to himself; and at his request I related my past misfortunes, the reason which brought me to Nantes, and my future prospects.

"'He heard me with attention, but strenuously opposed my leaving the kingdom—'If I live, Hilaire,' he said, 'you shall share my fortune: if I die— none but yourself shall inherit it.'

"'As I saw he wished it, I readily promised to remain with him; and from that day my time and attention were employed to effect his restoration: but my efforts, and those of the faculty, were equally ineffectual; he died in my arms, resigned and serene, leaving me, as he had promised, the undivided heir of his possessions.

"'I felt the loss of my brother more severely than might have been expected from the little time he had been known to me; but the tie of nature, never before indulged, joined to the lively regard he evinced for me, made me regret him as the dearest of friends: and as he had left me wealth beyond my wishes, I relinquished my intention of quitting France, and determined to dedicate the residue of my days to the service of my God, and the assistance of my fellow-creatures. In the course of settling my affairs, I came to Rennes, and here meeting with a companion of my boyish days, who had become a Benedictine, I determined to enter into the same brotherhood; and as soon as I had fully withdrawn my money from business, after vainly endeavouring to discover the generous Corbet, to repay my debt of gratitude, here took the cowl. Half my property I settled on the Convent, reserving the other at my own disposal, to relieve those I thought deserving my assistance.

"'And here, young man, I have experienced a foretaste of that happiness I hope to enjoy hereafter. I look forward with hope, I can look back without regret: I have experienced misfortunes, but never was guilty of an action, that can justly raise the blush of shame on my cheek!"

CHAPTER V.

"The worthy Monk," continued Sir Henry, "here concluded; and I bowed my head in conviction to the justness of the reproach his last words implied. As the good father intended, I could not avoid drawing a comparison of our lives; and the resignation, the fortitude he had evinced, indeed, raised a blush for the madness of which I had been guilty. The mention he made of my Louise, however, and the hope that, by means, I should be able to trace her, soon obliterated every unpleasant sensation; and, without disclosing my history or name, I informed him the infant he had mentioned was at that time the object of my search. I related the treatment I had met with at the convent of St. Ursule, and asked his advice as to the measures I should pursue to discover her. He was urgent to know who we were, but, on my telling him I was not at liberty to reveal what he asked, he desisted; and offered to go himself and speak to the Abbess concerning Louise. I thankfully accepted his offer, and, at his earnest solicitation, consented to take the sustenance I truly wanted.

"He was gone nearly an hour, and returned unsuccessful in his mission. Mother St. Brigide could not refuse to see him, though her answers were very unsatisfactory. She confessed that Louise had been reared in the Convent, but utterly disclaimed all knowledge of the lady who took her. She had not, she said, ever been admitted to the confidence of her predecessor; and the circumstance of Louise leaving the Convent had been both secret and sudden. Finding it impossible to gain the information he wanted, Father Hilaire returned to me. I received his account with a sigh, and declared my resolution to re-commence my search after Louise the ensuing morning. He approved my determination, and imperceptibly drew me into a conversation, as entertaining as instructive; and when we parted at night, gave me his blessing and a purse containing forty louis.

"The supply was seasonable. I parted from him with regret; and early the next morning left Rennes.

"For four months I wandered through Anjou, Poitou, and Bretagne, without meeting with any occurrence worthy of mention, or being able to trace Louise. When I rescued her from the Count, as I before observed, I did not see her face; and, unsuspicious of who she was, still continued my search; till my money being expended, and not knowing how to procure subsistence, I engaged in the vessel which conveyed me to St. Helena."

"The history of Father Hilaire," said the Captain, "is not without its moral; from the misfortunes of others, we are induced to draw a comparative consolation under our own; and his may truly teach the impatient sufferer an useful lesson."

"Yet I wish, Sir Henry," said Frederick, "you had informed him who you were; for, from the idea I have conceived of the man, I think he would have been highly gratified in repaying the obligation he owed your father."

"He had more than cancelled the obligation, Frederick," answered Sir Henry, "by preserving my life; and, had I acknowledged who I was, it might have led to questions I should have found it difficult and distressing to have answered."

The conversation here became general, and soon after they separated for the night.

The relation of Sir Henry added greatly to Louise's solicitude to be informed respecting her parents, but her inquiries and intreaties were equally ineffectual; Sir Henry persevered in his mysterious silence on the subject, though the anxiety she showed evidently added to his unhappiness; and, on their nearer approach to England, they with grief perceived in him every symptom of a rapid decline. The Captain in vain urged medical assistance; and, as he watched the daily ravages of sorrow, painfully anticipated the moment when death would bereave him of the friend by whose means he had hoped to recover his Ellenor. Frederick, independently of his concern on his uncle's account, regarded Sir Henry with more than fraternal friendship; but his eloquence was equally unavailing to discover the source from whence his unhappiness arose.

At last, the loud shouts of the sailors proclaimed the appearance of their native land, and in a few days they reached the Thames: thence Harland, impatient to introduce his Louise to his parents, proceeded to Harland-Hall; whilst the Captain, accompanied by Sir Henry and Frederick, pursued his way toward London, intending, as soon as he had transacted his business there, to renew his search after Ellenor; but in this he was prevented, by the arrival of one of Mrs. Howard's servants, who, the morning preceding the commencement of his intended search, hastily entered the room where he was at breakfast, and, presenting a letter, informed him his lady was at the point of death.

Alarmed at this intelligence, he eagerly opened the letter, which was from the steward, and confirmed the bearer's account, with entreaties that he would immediately repair to Bristol, where Mrs. Howard had for some time resided.—Humanity demanded compliance: the Captain accordingly set out with the messenger, and reached Bristol a few hours previously to Mrs. Howard's dissolution; but the malignancy which had ever marked her character displayed itself in her latest moments. She received the Captain with that acrimonious contempt which, for years, had accompanied each sentiment or look addressed to him. The loss of life she regretted, as depriving her of the power of longer tormenting him; and, with a smile of triumph that defied the power of death to efface, told him, she had left him her fortune, but on restriction that he never married again, as a punishment for his treatment of her.

The Captain could not affect a concern at her death which he did not experience; for years she had proved literally a torment; and he could not but feel that he was free: free to claim the promise of his Ellenor, and, in an union with her, meet a recompence for the years of unhappiness he had endured from Deborah, whose fortune, if requisite, he would not have hesitated a moment in resigning; but that lady's wishes had, in this respect, exceeded her power, for her fortune was fully secured to him at the time of their marriage.

The Captain wrote immediately for his nephew and Sir Henry, who arrived the day after the funeral; and, having settled his affairs with the steward, with every cheerful sentiment, hope could inspire, commenced his projected search for Ellenor and his son.—Neither was Frederick uninterested in the discovery of them; as the idea of the youthful Ellen was still impressed on his mind; and he secretly wished fortune had blessed him with independency, that he might have offered her his hand and heart. Sir Henry likewise seemed to forget his own sorrow, in the prospect of the Captain's happiness, and, by a number of little anecdotes concerning the objects of their search, endeavoured to beguile the time, and lessen the solicitude they could not altogether avoid experiencing.

They crossed the Channel to Cardiff, and directed their course to the humble dwelling of Jarvis, who, they thought, might, perhaps, by that time have learned the route of the fugitives.

The honest innkeeper received them with a hearty welcome, and, in answer to their inquiries, informed them, that a few weeks after they left the village, a man arrived there, who declared himself commissioned by Lieutenant Booyers, to dispose of the furniture of the cottage; which was accordingly sold: that Jarvis had endeavoured to learn where the Lieutenant had retired, but the man behaved with the greatest reserve. On his leaving the village, however, he had taken a guide to Newport, and by an inadvertent sentence he had uttered, he was induced to believe the Lieutenant and the ladies were gone to reside at—or near Gloucester. The Captain's heart beat with exulting hope at this intelligence; and such was his impatience to recover the lost partner of his heart, he would that instant have set out for Gloucester, could Sir Henry have supported the fatigue of such rapid travelling. On his account he consented to remain where they were till the morning, when Sir Henry willingly obeyed his summons to continue their journey.

Early the ensuing day, they reached Gloucester, where the Captain, Sir Henry, and Frederick, separated, to inquire through the city, agreeing to meet in the evening, at the inn where they left their horses. For two days they traversed the city, and, on the morning of the third, were preparing to leave the inn, to search some of the adjacent villages, when they were surprised by the appearance of Sir Arthur Howard. As the Captain had long ceased to regard him with enmity, he cordially advanced to meet him, whilst Frederick, forgetting his unkindness in the unexpected rencounter, as eagerly sprung to embrace him. Sir Arthur was equally surprised, though less pleased at beholding them; he, however, returned their salutation, and, at their request, accompanied them into the room they had quitted. He there answered to their inquiries respecting his family, and coldly expressed his approbation at the improvement seven years had made in the person and manners of Frederick. Sir Arthur in reality was rather chagrined than pleased at the graceful figure and deportment of his son, as they conveyed a reproach to himself, at the time they evinced the care and attention of the Captain to the duties which he, though a father, had neglected.

The Captain observed the displeasure depicted in his countenance, but, unconscious of the cause, sought relief from an unpleasant pause in the discourse, by asking the occasion of his being at Gloucester? The question was likewise a relief to Sir Arthur, as it afforded him an opportunity of venting his rising spleen.

"I came to recover a runaway," he replied, "who is endeavouring to disgrace the family to which she has the honour to belong: but severely shall she suffer for the fault she has committed!"

He then informed them, he had projected a match for his eldest daughter, not only suitable, but highly advantageous, as the gentleman possessed a noble independency, and had offered to take her without a portion: by which means the fortune of his eldest son would be considerably augmented; but that his daughter had objected to the union, and, on his threatening her, had privately left the Hall. That he pursued her to Gloucester, where, the preceding day, he had luckily overtaken her, and was going to order his carriage, to re-convey her home, when he was addressed by the Captain.

Frederick heard this account with concern; he well knew the harshness of his father's temper, and sincerely pitied his sister, whom he had not seen since the days of childhood. He now entreated he might have that satisfaction, and Sir Arthur, who knew not well how to refuse, was necessitated to comply: though he expressed his fear she would endeavour to elude his vigilance, and again escape; and concluded with an invective against children in general, for their wilfulness and disobedience. The entrance of his daughter saved his auditors the necessity of replying; her looks were pallid, and she approached with a timidity, which was rather increased than relieved, by the appearance of strangers. Frederick, however, soon recalled her recollection of a brother to whom she had in her infancy been particularly attached; yet she dared not yield to the pleasure she had in beholding him. Her father's eye still sternly expressed his anger; tears fell from her own; and folding her arms round the neck of Frederick, she wept in silence on his bosom.

Sir Henry, who had hitherto been a silent spectator, could not, unmoved, witness the distress of the amiable Theodosia; for every tear of pleasure occasioned by the presence of her brother, was evidently accompanied by one of sorrow at the treatment she received from her father; he therefore advanced to her, and, in the mildest accents, joined Frederick in his endeavours to soothe and cheer her. They at last succeeded: a faint smile played on her lips, she looked up, and spoke with some degree of confidence.

Sir Arthur observed Sir Henry's attentions, and learning from the Captain who he was, permitted his features to unbend from their usual severity. He was no stranger to Sir Henry's family, or the fortune possessed by his father; and, knowing he was an only son, concluded his possessions were equally the same. Sir Henry's attention, therefore, which proceeded entirely from commiseration, he beheld with satisfaction, as thinking them occasioned by a softer passion. Theodosia, too, appeared to listen to, and regard him with unusual pleasure; and he determined to encourage an acquaintance, as the Corbet possessions were superior to those of the suitor he had wished Theodosia to have accepted.

He now condescended to enter into conversation with Sir Henry: he regarded his brother and son with a look of greater cordiality; and declared his intention of remaining with them till the evening. The Captain, who sincerely wished to be reconciled to him, looked on the determination as arising from a return of fraternal friendship, and cheerfully acceded to his proposal of passing the day together: nor could Frederick conceal his delight at an appearance of regard he had never before experienced, and as flattering to himself as it was unexpected.

A half-suppressed sigh from Theodosia, reminded him of her unpleasant situation; and, regarding the moment as favourable, he ventured to intercede to Sir Arthur in her behalf: the Captain warmly seconded him: Sir Henry did not think himself authorised to speak; but the concern expressed in his countenance, and the glance of intercession he directed to Sir Arthur, pleaded more effectually in her cause, than the eloquence of Frederick and the Captain: as it erroneously added to his opinion, that Sir Henry was enamoured of his daughter. Pleased with the idea, he pretended to yield to intreaties, he would otherwise have disregarded; and not only pronounced Theodosia's pardon for her elopement, but promised to dismiss all thoughts of forcing her into an union with a man she avowedly disapproved. Theodosia could not speak her joy—her thanks at this unlooked-for indulgence; but, pressing her father's hand to her lips, burst into tears. Sir Arthur's bosom was a stranger to the milder virtues: he coldly reproved, what he termed, her childish behaviour; and, withdrawing his hand, bade her not abuse the forgiveness she had by no means merited; and remember that on her future behaviour must depend the continuance of his good opinion.

Theodosia felt the ungenerous chiding of her father, at a moment when her heart overflowed with the tenderest sentiments of filial gratitude and affection; she, however, knew him to be too tenacious of his word, to apprehend any farther importunity respecting her disagreeable lover; and the joy, which at first expressed itself in tears, soon restored the wonted smile to her animated countenance. Frederick beheld her returning cheerfulness with pleasure; whilst Sir Arthur, equally pleased with Sir Henry, and the chimerical idea he indulged of one day having him for a son-in-law, endeavoured to soften his natural austerity, and to conciliate the esteem of the interesting Corbet.

Early in the evening, as Sir Arthur had proposed, his carriage was in readiness, and he parted from his brother and son, with the greatest professions of friendship, pressing them, but more particularly Sir Henry, to pass some weeks at Howard Hall. The Captain, highly gratified at the occurrences of the day, readily accepted the invitation; and that night, for the first time during many years, experienced a repose, unembittered with the idea of a brother's hatred!

The next morning, he with his companions again continued his search after Ellenor, hope still leading them on to the reward the ensuing day might perhaps afford, to compensate for the disappointments of the one which had passed.

Already had they traversed great part of Gloucestershire, when in crossing from Painswick to Cheltenham, an equipage passed them, the unusual elegance of which attracted the Captain's attention. A lady, whose personal beauty, though on the wane, could be equalled by few, was in the principal carriage; and was so intently engaged in perusing a letter, that the party passed unheeded. The Captain was beginning to express his admiration, when he was alarmed by Sir Henry's falling from his horse, in a state of insensibility; from which their efforts to recover him proved ineffectual. A servant was, therefore, dispatched for assistance, and soon returned with a surgeon, to whose house Sir Henry was conveyed.

The Captain's concern at this accident was considerably increased, when he understood it might be attended with fatal consequences; and, not being willing to intrust the life of Sir Henry entirely to the skill of the surgeon, he sent to Gloucester for a physician, who, on visiting the patient, declared there was no immediate danger: the illness of Sir Henry proceeded from distress of mind; a confidential friend, he affirmed, was the most essential requisite toward his recovery; to which his native air might in some degree likewise conduce. To the surprise of the Captain, and regret of the surgeon, Sir Henry instantly coincided with the latter part of his advice, and as Ellenor, notwithstanding Jarvis's supposition, might have retired to Caermarthen, the Captain readily agreed to his proposal of proceeding to that county; and in spite of Sir Henry's feeble state, which would scarcely admit of his travelling, they, the next day, pursued their way toward Wales.

CHAPTER VI.

On entering an inn at Monmouth, the Captain was surprised at beholding Mr. Talton, who advanced to meet him with a hasty exclamation, expressive of the joy he felt at the rencounter. Far different were the sensations of Sir Henry; he could not regard Mr. Talton with composure; but, pressing the Captain's hand, bade him remember his promise, and immediately retired to his chamber.

Mr. Talton then inquired the particulars of Sir Henry's restoration, as he had heard an account of his visit to the parsonage, which was afterwards confirmed by the confession of old Owen, of his real existence: and, to the astonishment of the Captain, he learned it was Lady Corbet who had passed them near Painswick, and who, having been informed by Lady Dursley of her son's arrival, was then going to London, to entreat his return to Caermarthen. This instantly accounted to the Captain for Sir Henry's fainting, and his willingness to revisit Wales; he would not, however, comply with Mr. Talton's proposal to apprize Lady Corbet of their destination, that she might see her son: Sir Henry's will, in that respect, he said, should be uncontrolled; he had given his promise, and it should be sacred.

Mr. Talton at last ceased from further importunity; and finding the Captain proposed to stay at Monmouth only that night, expressed his regret at their early separation; accusing the Captain with want of friendship, in not deferring his journey at least for one day.

"Freely, Talton," said the Captain, "would I defer my journey a week, if it depended on myself; but, as I must think Sir Henry's life really in danger, notwithstanding the Physician's affirmation; let that plead my excuse.—Neither, I think, could you experience pleasure in our society; as Sir Henry's dislike—or, term it what you will—must place a restraint on every moment. I do not expect to leave England for some time; and if I recover my Ellenor, most probably shall quit the seafaring life; therefore, depend on it, I will shortly pay you a visit, when you shall find me neither a niggard of my time, nor forgetful of the sentiments I once avowed."

With this assurance Mr. Talton was obliged to retire for the night; but in the morning renewed his solicitations: in which not being able to prevail, he declared he would postpone his journey to London, and return with the Captain to the interior of Wales.

Sir Henry turned pale at this declaration, which Mr. Talton observing, said—"I perceive with sorrow, Sir Henry, the early prepossession you entertained against me is not eradicated; perhaps from mistaking the cause of your conduct, I have acted toward you with a severity foreign to my nature, but which I thought highly authorised by reason! Your reserve to me, on the renewal of my acquaintance with your mother, I imputed, I acknowledge, to interested motives. That I love Lady Corbet, is no secret to you; but that I wished to alienate her fortune—nothing was ever farther from my thoughts! On the contrary, if your amiable mother bless me with her hand, it is my avowed, my earnest wish, that the estates appertaining to the Corbet family, should be resigned to you. My fortune is more than adequate to my wants or desires: and Heaven forbid that I should be instrumental in withholding from you those possessions, of which the injustice of your father would deprive you."

Sir Henry sighed, and Mr. Talton, after a moments pause, proceeded.—"Your mother has consented to resign the name of Corbet, when her son can be prevailed on to return: but whilst he is a wanderer, she cannot experience happiness. Thus, Sir Henry, you see the claims which are made upon you. Your mother's happiness, consequently mine—and I must think your own—depend on your compliance. I, therefore, again entreat your return to the seat of your ancestors; let these seeming mysteries be cleared up, and, by giving me a legal title to the name of father, let me compensate for him you have lost!"

Sir Henry appeared agitated, and, taking the hand of Mr. Talton, "I believe, Mr. Talton, I have mistaken your character. Your affection for my mother I am no stranger to; and sincerely wish it depended but on me to ensure your happiness: but, alas! the means would prove the bane! I will, however, see—will speak to my mother: more I dare not promise; and for that—I may, perhaps, answer with my life!"

Mr. Talton and the Captain regarded Sir Henry with a momentary astonishment—"Your life!" repeated the former—But Sir Henry bowed, and taking Frederick by the arm, left the room.

"May answer with his life!" reiterated Mr. Talton. "What, Howard, can he mean?"

The Captain could not resolve the question, and, after a few unsatisfactory surmises, they followed Sir Henry and Frederick, who were already on horseback. Sir Henry's reply, however, had given rise to such a confusion of ideas in the mind of Mr. Talton, he could by no means reconcile them; he therefore asked an explanation: but Sir Henry's answers tended only to increase the mystery.

In the afternoon, willing to avoid the revival of the subject, he lingered behind with Frederick; whilst the Captain and Mr. Talton, being engaged in a discourse highly interesting to the former, as it concerned his Ellenor, were not aware of the separation till they had gained the summit of a hill, where, on turning round, the Captain perceived them and their attendants nearly two miles behind. He immediately proposed to wait for them, and, retiring beneath the shade of an oak, began to descant on the prospect before them, which presented one of the richest scenes of autumn.

The non-appearance of Sir Henry and Frederick, however, soon recalled their attention from the beauties of nature; and the Captain, declaring his apprehension that some accident had happened, with every mark of impatient concern, descended the hill, followed by Mr. Talton and his servant. Their party, however, was not to be perceived. They had, indeed, taken a road, which led in a different direction from the bottom of the hill, and which the Captain now first observed. Anxious to overtake them, he hastened the pace of his horse, but no appearance of them could be discovered; and the road branching off into a variety of others, added to his perplexity. In this dilemma, he followed the advice of Mr. Talton, and entered that which, from its direction, they supposed would lead to Brecon: but it soon became so intricate, that they at last agreed to relinquish the attempt, and endeavour to trace their way back.

This, however, they found as difficult to accomplish, nor was it till night had spread her glooms over the surrounding scenes, that they entered a road, which, from the plainness of its tracks, they imagined to be the one they had formerly quitted. Mr. Talton could not refrain from a hasty exclamation against the young men, for their carelessness: which was answered by expressions of concern on their account by the Captain.

Slowly they ascended the hill; when, to the consternation of Mr. Talton, he discovered they had entirely mistaken their road: they had, however, no alternative, but to proceed, trusting to Providence for guidance; and continued their way, till they arrived at a place where the road again taking different directions, involved them in their former perplexity.

"What is now to be done?" asked Mr. Talton. "By Heavens, I think some dæmon has placed a spell in our path, to mislead and confound us! Fools that we were, to travel without a guide!"

"The road was sufficiently plain," answered the Captain, "if we had not negligently missed it. But hark! I think I hear the trampling of horses. If it be Sir Henry and my nephew, I shall think little of passing the night under the canopy of Heaven: and in the morning we may easily rectify our mistake."

He listened attentively; but, two horsemen only approached: he, however, hailed them, and on being answered, briefly recounted the manner in which he had been separated from his nephew, his subsequent search, and the unpleasant situation he was then in, begging to know if they had accidentally seen the objects of his anxiety, or would direct him to some hamlet or town, where he and his friend might procure accommodations for the night?

"I am sorry, Sir," said the stranger, who had first answered the Captain's salutation, "it is not in my power to give you any intelligence respecting your friends. In regard to a night's lodging, it is at least three miles to the next village, whence I now come, and the road is very indifferent; I reside about half a mile from this place, and if you will accompany me home, although I cannot promise you splendid entertainment, I can insure you a hearty welcome."

Pleased with the frankness of the offer, the Captain and Mr. Talton accepted it, and, turning their horses, followed the benevolent stranger. The uncertainty, however, of Frederick's and Sir Henry's safety, destroyed the momentary satisfaction of the Captain, nor could he help expressing his fears to the stranger.

"Hope for the best, Sir," he replied: "my humble dwelling, though screened on this side from observation, commands an extensive view over the lower part of the country; where, from your account, I am induced to think your friends have strayed: and whence the light from our window will most probably serve them as a guide."

"May it prove a favourable beacon!" said the Captain. "Yonder is the place of our destination," continued the stranger, extending his hand toward a distant light.

"Aye—and there, Sir," said his attendant, "is Argus barking most furiously. What, in the name of wonder, can ail the beast? Surely the house is not beset by thieves."

The stranger stopped his horse for a moment, and listened—the barking continued without intermission, and a distant shout likewise assailed their ears.

"Something, I am afraid, has indeed happened," he cried in a voice of concern. "If you please, gentlemen, we will hasten forward."

The shouts increased, mixed with the deep-mouthed tones of Argus: but not as they had apprehended, in a direction from the house. They, however, still hastened forward.—"It may be our fugitives," said the Captain.—"Ah! I hear Frederick's voice!" He now exerted his own, and in a few minutes, was joined by the wanderers.

"Thank heaven, my dear uncle, we have found you!" said Frederick exultingly—"a circumstance, from the various accidents we have met with, beyond my hopes. But for this noble dog, we should most probably yet have been in a morass, we incautiously entered."

The Captain could scarcely express his concern at the difficulties they had experienced, ere they arrived at the gateway, leading to the ancient though not extensive dwelling of the hospitable stranger. An aged man-servant attended the summons of his master: Sir Henry started on beholding him, and, anxiously grasping the Captain's arm, cried—"O gracious Heaven!—haste, haste, Captain!" and hurrying him past their kind invitor, entered the house.—The Captain had not time to ask the meaning of his behaviour, before Sir Henry, with a trembling hand, threw open the door of a parlour.

A cheerful fire blazed on the hearth, round which were seated a gentleman, a lady, and two lovely girls.

"Is that my Edward?" the lady asked; and, raising her head, discovered to the Captain, the features of his Ellenor!

"My Ellenor!" he exclaimed, rushing to her, "Yes, it is your Edward! my loved—my long-lost Ellenor!"

A scream of surprise and delight escaped her as he caught her in his arms, and faintly articulating his name, she sunk inanimate on his bosom.

Mrs. Blond, who had been engaged in an adjoining room, alarmed by the scream, flew to the assistance of her friend, at the moment Mr. Talton, Frederick, and young Howard, entered the room: but the appearance of the former, in an instant obliterated every other idea, and, wildly clasping her hands, she stood the image of horror!

"My mother!—Do I once more behold you?" said Sir Henry, hastening to meet her—but she heeded him not, her eye was fixed on Talton: nor was it till the repeated exclamation of—"Sir Henry! my benefactor!" roused her from her stupor. Franticly she threw her arms round Sir Henry; but Talton again attracting her eye, she as hastily pushed him from her, crying—"Fly—fly, my Harry; destruction awaits thee! It is Talton himself. Fly to Howard, he only can protect thee! Oh! Ellenor—Ellenor, ruin awaits us all."

The surprise which had been depicted on the countenance of Mr. Talton, now yielded to embarrassment, as his name was faintly echoed on every side: Sir Henry vainly attempted to persuade them Talton was not an enemy: Mrs. Blond still urged him to fly, till overpowered by the agitation of her mind, she sunk in a state of insensibility on the floor.

All was incoherence and confusion: the friendly Booyers had been assisting the Captain and young Howard, to restore Ellenor to life; he now ran distractedly from her to Mrs. Blond, in vain calling for help: the entrance of the servants but added to the distress which prevailed.

At last the Captain, with joy perceived the current of life re-animate the features of his Ellenor; who, in a few minutes, became conscious of her situation. With a smile of inexpressible delight, she took the hand of her son, and placing it in that of the Captain, encircled them in her arms. The action spoke more than words; nature confessed it: Edward intuitively bent his knee, and as the Captain raised, and pressed him to his heart, he felt that moment more than recompensed for all he had suffered.

A faint groan from Mrs. Blond now reached the ear of Ellenor, and, leaving her Edward, she flew to the side of this companion in her afflictions: but her attentions were equally unavailing to recall her senses, and she was therefore conveyed to her chamber, followed by her daughter and Ellen. Ellenor would likewise have attended, but was prevented by Sir Henry, who, affectionately taking her hand, was beginning to congratulate her on her restoration to the Captain, when the door was again thrown open, and the old servant-man rushed into the room.

"It is—it is Sir Henry!" he exclaimed, throwing himself at his feet. "Little did I think, when I opened the gate, it was to admit the son of my beloved master. Yet my old eyes could not distinguish you: but since the news arrived that you were drowned, they have been more dim than they were wont to be! Ah! many a tear has been shed for your loss, my master; and as often have I wished, I could have recalled your life, by resigning my own."

"I thank you, my good old friend," said Sir Henry, raising him; "sincerely thank you for your love: and may one day have it in my power to acknowledge it more effectually, than by words; though, for myself, Thomas, the tomb of my father is the only inheritance I covet!"

His head drooped on his bosom, whilst the starting tear too plainly evinced the painful recollection of the moment. With looks of the tenderest pity, Ellenor folded him in her arms.

"Forgive me," continued Sir Henry, returning her embrace. "At such a moment as this, I ought not to let a single idea of myself intrude, to cast a gloom on your happiness. For your sake—for the sake of my beloved Eliza, and her mother, I will break through those ties, which have hitherto restrained me, and act according to the dictates of justice!"

"The means are in our power!" cried old Thomas, exultingly. "The night before my Lady returned from London, with the account of your death, I entered the closet of my deceased master; the event answered our expectation: and now let the guilty beware!"

Sir Henry sighed; but in a moment assuming a more cheerful aspect, reminded Thomas, they were weary travellers, who, for some hours had not received refreshment.

Thomas instantly left the room; and Sir Henry congratulated the Captain and his Ellenor on the late happy discovery. Young Howard and Lieutenant Booyers likewise claimed his attention; he introduced them to Frederick and Mr. Talton, who, already prepossessed in their favour, eagerly accepted, and returned their proffered friendship. The name of Talton caused a momentary alarm in the bosom of Ellenor: involuntarily she threw herself into the arms of the Captain, for protection; but, on his assuring her of Talton's friendship, apologized for her mistrust, and extending her hand, welcomed him with all the cordiality she had formerly shown.

"I believe, Mrs. Crawton," said Mr. Talton, "my appearance here is as surprising to you, as the events of this evening have been to me. Some strange mistake exists; but as an explanation is beyond my power, I can only assert my innocence of intentional wrong toward you, or your friends!"

"No more apologies, Talton," said the Captain; "let the past be forgotten; for your conduct in future, I will be answerable; and, as the first proof of your friendship, shall demand your attendance again on my Ellenor, as a father.— Your Howard," he continued to Ellenor, "is, thank Heaven, at last at liberty, and here claims your promise, of again uniting your fate to his for ever!"

A tear of grateful delight swelled in the eye of Ellenor, as she gave him her hand, and assured him her promise was not forgotten.

The entrance of Ellen and Eliza, with the account that Mrs. Blond was fallen into a gentle sleep, added to their satisfaction: "And as I was anxious," said Ellen with a smile, "to see my adopted brother, I persuaded Eliza to leave her mother to the sweets of repose, and return with me to our friends."

A blush overspread the beautiful face of her companion, as Sir Henry said— "And did Eliza require persuasion, to return to the presence of her Henry? A welcome from her was the first wish of my heart, and is she then the last to give it?"

"Do more justice to the sentiments of Eliza," said young Howard.—"Deeply has she mourned the loss of Corbet; and her heart, I am certain, if not her tongue, sincerely welcomes, and rejoices at his return."

Sir Henry pressed the hand of the blushing girl to his lips, and, with a heart more replete with happiness than he had long experienced, attended the summons to the supper-table. The restraint which the presence of Mr. Talton at first created, gradually wore off; as, willing to eradicate the idea he was certain they entertained of him, he exerted those powers of pleasing, which he possessed in an eminent degree; and on their retiring for the night, each secretly wished he might prove himself as amiable as he had that evening appeared to be.

CHAPTER VII.

Early in the morning, the Captain rose, and having dispatched his servant to Monmouth for a licence, left the house for the purpose of enjoying a ramble, till the appearance of his Ellenor; but had not proceeded many paces, when he perceived his son, Sir Henry, and Frederick. He immediately joined them, and, under the guidance of Edward, traced the tangled wilds, which had afforded an asylum to his Ellenor.

"It is now more than eighteen months," said young Howard, "since the appearance of Mr. Talton drove us from the house of Lieutenant Booyers, whither we had retired on the report of Sir Henry's death. Not knowing which way to direct our steps, and uncertain whether, in flying from one evil, we were not hurrying into a greater, we pursued an indirect road to Monmouth; where, leaving my mother and Mrs. Blond, I set out with our faithful Thomas, in search of an obscure village, or cot, that might afford us the shelter we required.

"Fortune conducted me to this spot, which was then in the wildest state of ruin. The beauties which surrounded it, and its retired situation, immediately pointed it out as a place designed by Heaven to afford the asylum we wanted. The owner, for a trifling consideration, agreed to my becoming his tenant, and here we removed the whole of our property, not amounting to a hundred pounds.—Industry, however, found out many means of procuring a livelihood: needle-work, embroidery, painting, every accomplishment was turned to account, and, with superintending our household affairs, employed the time of my mother and her friends.

"Thomas, before he entered the service of Sir Horace Corbet, had been engaged in the farming business; and under his direction, your Edward, my dear Sir, set his hand to the plough and spade; nor was our friendly Booyers idle; though deprived of an arm, he assisted in sowing, pruning, &c. and under his care, the garden soon assumed a pleasing and flourishing appearance.—On our first coming, we engaged an useful active man, who lived in the only cottage near our residence; and who, from his knowledge of the land, directed, as well as executed, our first plans of husbandry: his wife likewise superintends our dairy, who, with Susan, comprise the female attendants of our family. This man, we sent, as being unknown, to dispose of the furniture left in the residence we had so abruptly deserted: and he executed his commission with the greatest exactness; leaving the village, as we had directed, by a different route from the one he was really to pursue; by which means, we hoped to avoid being traced. Our house was soon repaired: and our harvest, though late, richly repaid our labour. Plenty, indeed, has here deigned to dwell; and, could we have forgotten the past, we might have been happy; but remembrance still recalled the friends we had lost, and, by a retrospect of the injuries we had suffered, cast a shade on the passing moment."

"But what, my son," said the Captain, "are the injuries to which you allude?"

The appearance of Mr. Talton and Lieutenant Booyers, prevented Edward from replying; and, on being joined by those gentlemen, the conversation was renewed on general subjects, till they arrived at the spot where the Captain had the preceding evening met with his son; when Mr. Talton said,—"I yesterday, Howard, should have treated the idea with the greatest ridicule, that the accidents we met with, could be the means of conducting us to Mrs. Crawton, or that by losing our way, you should meet with a son, you have so many years vainly sought.—But under your present embarrassments," he continued, addressing Edward, "do you think, young gentleman, you acted prudently in inviting two strangers to your house? Had Talton been the man you suspected, it might have been attended with unpleasant circumstances. But it was benevolence which impelled you, and it has been rewarded!"

"Or rather, Sir," said Edward smiling, "it was nature; which, the moment my father spoke, attached me to him, and destroyed the caution, which the situation of our affairs certainly required."

"Providence," said Frederick, "equally guided us all. By deviating from our road yesterday, we saved the life of a man and his son; who, in crossing a foot-bridge, by the heedlessness of the boy, fell into the current beneath. We likewise had the satisfaction of relieving a family, reduced to the lowest state of poverty and distress. These circumstances detained us a considerable time; and afforded such ample scope for conversation, that all remembrance of you and Mr. Talton was lost; and it was not till the close of day, you recurred to our recollection. Willing then to rectify the error we had committed, we took the nearest direction toward Brecon; but had not proceeded far, before Sir Henry's horse sunk into a morass; and in endeavouring to assist him, my own met with the same fate. This completed our distress; and by the time we had succeeded in extricating the unlucky animals, darkness had nearly enveloped the heavens. We would then have retraced our path, but could not discover it; and fearful of wandering from the spot where we were, we hallooed for assistance, but without effect; and I began to have very disagreeable ideas, when we were relieved by Argus, who sprung to Sir Henry, with the familiarity of an old acquaintance, enticing us to follow him; nor did we deliberate long, but, tying a handkerchief to his collar, submitted ourselves to his guidance. He soon conducted us to a firm road, and we were directing our steps toward the light, which beamed from the windows of our friends, when you, my dear uncle, so happily joined us."

They were here interrupted by the arrival of a servant, with a summons to breakfast, and, on entering the parlour, they had the satisfaction of seeing Mrs. Blond, assembled with the rest of the family. Sir Henry instantly flew to her, and affectionately welcomed her return to their society.

"The happiness of my friend Ellenor, and the discovery of your existence," said Mrs. Blond, faintly smiling, "have been my restoratives; to see the child of my beloved Corbet; to know that the means of obtaining him justice, are in our possession—O, Harry, I cannot speak my joy!"

They proceeded to breakfast, and the Captain, at Ellenor's request, related the occurrences of his life, since their separation, and the little train of accidents which had conducted him to her. "And now, my Ellenor," he continued, "will you gratify my impatience, and explain a mystery, which for years has perplexed and rendered me unhappy?"

"As I live, there are Harland and Louise!" interrupted Sir Henry, as a carriage drove to the gate; and, hastening out of the room, he immediately introduced his sister and the Lieutenant. An exclamation of surprise escaped Mr. Talton, as Sir Henry presented her to him, but passed unheeded, as the Captain asked Harland, by what accident he had discovered where they were?

"By unexpectedly meeting your servant, Captain," answered Harland.—"We have for some weeks been engaged in a ramble through the adjacent parts, and were this morning going to Brecon, when we met James. He instantly informed us where you were, and of some farther particulars, which induced us to use the privilege of relationship, and join Sir Henry.

"Welcome, indeed," said Ellenor, "shall the relations of my Henry ever be. The countenance of Louise is a passport to the heart; nor is there one here, who could refuse her a claim to their friendship."

Louise looked wistfully at Ellenor; the strong resemblance between her and Sir Henry, the cordiality of her salutation, gave rise to the idea, that it might perhaps be the mother she so ardently wished to know, who embraced her. The name of mother faintly escaped her lips, as her inquiring eye glanced to Sir Henry, for a confirmation of her suspicion.

"No, my sweet girl," replied Sir Henry, "this Lady is not your mother; would to Heaven thine were equally amiable! This morning, Louise, is dedicated to the explanation of my life and conduct; and fortunately are you arrived to learn the particulars of your birth without necessitating me to repeat a tale, which will distress you equally to hear, as me to relate."

"I was early taught resignation to the will of Heaven, my brother," replied Louise; "nor will I shrink from the recital; though happy should I have deemed myself, if I had here found a mother!"

"In affection you shall, sweet girl," said Ellenor; "Louise is not answerable for the vices of her parents!"

The Captain here introduced his Ellenor and son, more particularly to Harland and Louise; who congratulated them on their restoration to each other; and after they had partaken of refreshments, the Captain reminded Sir Henry of the expected relation.

"Yet, before I commence my narrative," said Sir Henry, "let me explain the meaning of a sentence, you say has occasioned you so much anxiety—the secret to which your Ellenor in her letter alluded.

"In Ellenor Worton, then, give me leave to introduce the daughter of Sir Horace Corbet—the sister of my father! Worton was the name she received from her god-mother, and which she wholly assumed, when the harshness of Sir Horace drove her from her paternal roof; and when she discovered, that her Howard had been previously married, she regarded it as a punishment for her breach of filial obedience. Suspend your surprise a moment.—In Mrs. Blond, behold the youngest daughter of Sir James Elvyn:—another victim of my grandfather's cruelty and injustice!"

"Good God!" cried Mr. Talton: "And does your mother, Sir Henry, know of these circumstances?"

"She does, Mr. Talton," answered Sir Henry, with a sigh. The Captain's looks likewise testified his surprise.—"But wherefore, my Ellenor," he said, "the necessity of concealing your name from my knowledge?"

"With the character of my father, Howard," answered Ellenor, "you have already been made acquainted. Proud, vindictive, and avaricious, every consideration yielded to the gratification of those passions. On account of her fortune, he married my mother, to whom he proved literally a tyrant: nor did his children experience greater affection or indulgence. When I was seventeen, old Lord Aberford, who had accidentally seen me, declared himself my admirer; and as his offers were highly gratifying to my father, he little regarded sacrificing my happiness. In vain were my tears, my mother's intreaties, or the supplications of my brother: fury took possession of his bosom, at our daring to dispute his will; and in the first paroxysm of rage, he sent my mother to a ruinous seat he possessed in Cornwall, ordered my brother back to college, and confined me to my chamber; which he vowed I should never leave, till he resigned me to the arms of Lord Aberford. The being separated from my mother, was the severest punishment he could inflict, as her tenderness ever compensated for the harshness of his behaviour.

"His increasing severity, every time he visited my apartment, had nearly reduced me to compliance, when Thomas returned from Cornwall, and secretly delivered me a letter from my mother. She advised me, if my father still persisted in forcing me into an union with Lord Aberford, to leave the Hall, and seek an asylum at Mrs. Radnor's, the bosom friend of her early days. The means of escape were easily effected by Thomas, who at night placed a ladder at my window, and conducted me in safety to the park-gate, whence Owen, the gamekeeper, who was waiting with horses, escorted me to Radnor Moor.—Mrs. Radnor received me with open arms, and, fully aware of the violent temper of my father, advised my taking the name of Worton; and, to screen me more effectually from his knowledge, a few days after left the Moor for Brighthelmstone.

"I there, Howard, became acquainted with you. The sentiments we entertained for each other, were reciprocal; and freely should I have communicated the secret of my family, but Mrs. Radnor strenuously opposed it. Her detestation of my father, daily increased, and as he had declared that he no longer regarded me as his daughter, I should not, she said, with her approbation, ever acknowledge him as a father. The favourable opinion she entertained of you, encouraged the passion I had imbibed, and, regarding her councils as those of a parent, I early avowed my affection and consented to plight my faith to you for ever.

"At this time, my brother privately visited us. My father, he said, continued inveterate against me, and having discovered that my mother had been the instigator of my elopement, he still confined her at his estate in Cornwall, though he occasionally allowed my brother the liberty of seeing her. Henry brought me a letter, the last I ever received from my beloved mother. It was dictated by maternal tenderness. The happiness of her children, she said, constituted hers: Henry's, she thought, would be established in his expected union with Miss Elvyn; and mine, she hoped, would be equally secured, in the choice I had made. She added a blessing on our nuptials; and the morning after Henry left us, to join his friend Booyers, previously to his intended marriage, I gave my hand to you at the altar.

"Happy, indeed, were the days which succeeded our union, till the illness of Mrs. Radnor; which was occasioned by the sudden disclosure of my mother's death: her own followed in a few days, and I had to mourn the loss of both, and the knowledge I then first received of a brother's unhappiness.

"Gladly would I have flown to the bosom of my Edward, for consolation; but Mrs. Radnor had extorted a promise from me, not to undeceive you.—'If Crawton, my child,' she said, 'should find that you have acted disingenuously by him, it may implant suspicion in his mind, and destroy the tenderness you at present experience. Rest satisfied, then, my love, with the happiness you enjoy, nor hazard its destruction by that which cannot possibly increase it. If I advise wrong, may Heaven forgive me; but I speak from the best of motives.'

"Ah! she knew not the heart of Howard, or the precaution had been needless. What passed from that time, Edward, till the discovery of your prior marriage, I need not repeat: and what I experienced at that moment, is beyond my power to describe! An idea of self-destruction took possession of my mind, till the remembrance of my infant checked my despair; when, finding Susan willing to follow my fortune, I determined on flight. Your absence favoured my design; and leaving a few lines for you, with Mary, I proceeded to London.

"I was there delivered of my Edward, and as soon as I was enabled to bear the fatigue of travelling, proceeded to Caermarthen; where I sent a peasant to the Hall, and a few hours after had the satisfaction of beholding my brother.

"But ah, what an alteration had two years made in the once blooming, and ever interesting Corbet! All indeed was changed, but the heart of Henry!

"He wept over the sorrows of his Ellenor, promised to prove a father to my babe, and a protector to me: but, starting from his seat, he exclaimed, 'O God! vain is the promise!—Your father, Ellenor, has deprived me of the power. To revenge your refusal of Lord Aberford, he has cut you off from every part of his fortune; and prohibited my affording you the least pecuniary assistance, under forfeiture of every part of my property, but that entailed from my ancestors. Yet, think not, Ellenor, I can desert you: no, though I cannot publicly support you as my sister, I still will prove myself a brother!'

"Till that moment I knew not the death of my father: tears relieved my oppressed heart, and Henry, again embracing me, continued—'Grieve not, my sister; your father, in his last moments, wished he had been less severe; blessed his Ellenor, and prayed she might find a better friend than he had proved. He would have altered his will, but death prevented him: and your brother must ever be subjected to the control of—.'

"He paused—Alas! my brother, I knew not then the full extent of your misery!

"He that evening conducted me to the house of Mr. Blond, where for seventeen years I lived secluded from the world. The occurrences which then drove me from Caermarthen, will be fully recounted in the narrative of our Henry."

"Thanks, my dear Ellenor," said the Captain, "for your part of these explanations. It indeed shows me, by what trifles the happiness or misery of life may be occasioned. For a farther and final explanation, Sir Henry, we must now refer to you."

"The task," said Sir Henry, "is indeed a painful one: as it must discover the vices of a parent—nature still forces me to love!" He paused a moment, when, perceiving all were attentive, he began his relation, in the following words.

END OF VOLUME II.

Milton Keynes UK
Ingram Content Group UK Ltd.
UKHW012315040624
443649UK00020B/640

9 789361 470202